ARLENE
ON THE
SCENE

CAROL LIU

WITH MARYBETH SIDOTI CALDARONE

ARLENE ON THE SCENE

Carol *MSC*

"LIVE IT"

EMERALD
BOOK CO.

Published by Emerald Book Company
Austin, TX
www.emeraldbookcompany.com

Distributed by Emerald Book Company

For ordering information or special discounts for bulk purchases, please contact Emerald Book Company at PO Box 91869, Austin, TX 78709, 512.891.6100.

Design and composition by Greenleaf Book Group LLC and Publications Development Company
Cover design by Greenleaf Book Group LLC
Cover illustration by Mark Minnig

Publisher's Cataloging-In-Publication Data
(Prepared by The Donohue Group, Inc.)

Liu, Carol.
  Arlene on the scene / Carol Liu with Marybeth Sidoti Caldarone. -- 1st ed.

    p. ; cm.

    Summary: Arlene knows what it's like to be different. But in her quest to become the youngest student government officer in Greenwood Elementary history, she finally realizes the value in embracing differences.
    Interest age level: 006-012.
    ISBN: 978-1-934572-54-2

    1. Charcot-Marie-Tooth disease--Patients--Juvenile fiction. 2. Individuality--Juvenile fiction. 3. Student government--Elections--Juvenile fiction. 4. Individuality--Fiction. 5. Student government--Elections--Fiction. I. Caldarone, Marybeth Sidoti. II. Title.

PZ7.L5832 Ar 2010
[Fic]   2010928160

Part of the Tree Neutral™ program, which offsets the number of trees consumed in the production and printing of this book by taking proactive steps, such as planting trees in direct proportion to the number of trees used: www.treeneutral.com.

Printed in the United States of America on acid-free paper

10 11 12 13 14 15   10 9 8 7 6 5 4 3 2 1

First Edition

This book is lovingly dedicated to
Grace Caldarone

CONTENTS

BREAKING THE RULES

It was in fourth grade that I first arrived on the scene wearing my custom-made, bright purple leg braces decorated with floating butterflies.

Kids, teachers, even the janitors sure took long stares at me with these new things on my legs. Maybe the purple was just too much. Suddenly everyone could tell just by looking at me that I was different. It felt weird. I mean, imagine wearing a sign on your back that says, "I have trouble reading," or "I never learned how to ride a bike." It's like part of you is just *out there,* for everyone to see.

Before the school year started, I wondered what kids would think of me when I showed up for fourth grade. Would they just figure I broke both my legs? Would they realize I was still the same old Arlene? Would they like the butterfly decorations I picked out?

I wasn't positive about the answers to these questions, so I had to do something to make sure I could pick up where I left off before I got these braces. Near the end of the summer, I made plans—Big Plans. I was going to pop back onto the scene, like with a big "Ta-da!" And I would speed ahead with my Big Plans so fast that the sign on my back saying "Girl with the Leg Braces" would just fly off, disappearing into the wind forever.

Then my braces wouldn't be such a big deal, and I wouldn't be so different, like my mom is. She uses a wheelchair to get around. Everyone always makes a big fuss about her wheelchair. One time last year, in the auditorium, when Mom tried to sit in the aisle near the stage for a school play, some lady told her that she'd have to move because she was blocking the exit route. If there was a fire, the lady said, it would be too hard to get around her. So Mom had to sit way in the back, where she couldn't even see anything.

I didn't really get it. If a fire was burning down the school, wouldn't Mom be trying to get out too? She wouldn't just be sitting there, singing "La la la" and blocking the aisle. No way did I want that kind of attention on my leg braces. I'm a kid, not a fire hazard!

No, this year I was going to jump in and do something really impressive, something to stop anyone from thinking that I was any different from last year. I had thought a lot about what this awesome, impressive thing could be. Captain of the soccer team? Nope, can't run fast enough. Dancing Queen? No chance. Even with these braces wrapped around my calves and ankles, I'm still too wobbly. Ms. Smarty Pants? Well, I do pretty good in school, but not that good!

Then it hit me. I'm really good at talking with all kinds of people, and I'm always involved with school stuff, like the Book Fair and Playground Clean-Up Day. Chatting with people, showing up at events, working on projects—sure, I could be a politician!

In order to get going with my Big Plans, though, I needed the help of Mr. Musgrove, our principal. So I made an appointment to see him just a few weeks after school began. I think I surprised him when I walked into his office. He looked down at the schedule on his desk, then back up at me, and then back down at his schedule, like he was all confused or something.

"Shouldn't you be in class?" he asked.

"It's my recess time," I said. Didn't he know this?

He smiled a twinkly smile, with the lights reflecting off of his white teeth and his bald head. His big glasses were so clean I could see my face in them. I wanted to wave at myself, but I figured that would get us both off track, and I had only so much recess time left.

"Well, what brings you here, young lady?"

I cleared my throat, started talking, and my thoughts just fell out of my brain all at once. "Mr. Musgrove, I want to run for office in the Student Government Association this year, even though usually only fifth and sixth graders run, and I'm only in fourth grade, but I think I can do a great job, so can I please run for an SGA office? Is there, like, a strict rule about who can run, or could we maybe work something out?"

I knew I should have practiced my opening speech more. That felt a little jumbled up. I sucked in my breath and waited for his answer.

Mr. Musgrove chuckled. "Arlene, you're right. Only fifth and sixth graders can run for office, and it is indeed a rule. I'm sorry. Why can't you just run next year?"

"Well . . ." I had to think quickly. I couldn't say, "Because this is part of my grand entrance into fourth grade so that nobody makes a big deal about my leg braces." I didn't think Mr. Musgrove would really understand all that. So I blurted out the first reason that sprang into my head. "Because you made three kinds of officers: president, treasurer, and secretary. I want to be all of them, so I need three years to work with." I finished with a nod. There. That should do it.

Mr. Musgrove shook his head slowly. "I'm sorry, Arlene, but I think you need a year to get back into the swing of things. Your parents told me that you'll have to do lots of therapy now to keep your legs and arms strong, and they said you might feel more tired than you used to. If you take on too much right away this year, you could get really worn out.

I'm worried about you, Arlene, about your health and how you'll feel."

I sighed. It was already starting, people thinking of me like I'm some poor, weak little kid. My Big Plans—ruined before I even got going! "Please, Mr. Musgrove, please. This is really, really important to me."

Mr. Musgrove folded his hands on top of his desk and shook his head again. His voice was soft, but his words were sharp. "There's a rule for a reason, Arlene. Most fourth graders would find it hard to win a school-wide election. And for you, given the extra challenges you have this year, I'm afraid it'll just be a big disappointment."

"But Mr. Musgrove, I'm not asking you to make me win the election. I'm asking you to let me try!"

My heart was beating really fast, like it was trying to pump courage through all the veins in my body. I looked straight at my principal, like for a whole minute. I figured if I could just stare him down, maybe he would cave in. But he just looked right back at me, and his face didn't change.

It was already too late. I was already too different. My chin fell to my chest. I pushed my fists against my eyes as my mind raced in circles, trying to think of something else to say to change his mind.

I couldn't come up with anything, so I raised my head. Mr. Musgrove was still staring at me, with his head at a tilt and his cheek resting on his hand. I could almost hear the "Awww" ringing in his brain.

I watched Mr. Musgrove as he looked at my face, then down at my braces, and then back at my face again. My grandmother looks at me like this sometimes, like she's proud but also a little sad.

Yup, Mom told me about this look, how some people might feel sorry for me once they see my braces. She didn't say what to do about it, though.

Maybe there was a way to use this whole sympathy thing to get Mr. Musgrove to give me a chance.

But is that even OK to do?

I wasn't sure, but I did know that everything was riding on his answer.

MY LIFE + DISEASE

The next day began with one of those misty Rhode Island mornings, when the ocean tosses a little of itself into the sky, and then the wind sprinkles this salty coolness all over my neighborhood. I was kind of hoping for a bright and sunny day, to match how I felt. But as my dad, who was born in Rhode Island, explained, it's often gray and cool here because we live so close to the water. I just figured that since this is the smallest state, the sun sometimes forgets to stop by.

I was waiting at the bus stop, and although it was still September, I was shivering a little in my jacket. But I felt good about my conversation with Mr.

Musgrove the day before. When he got that sympathy look on his face, I did a little pout to help him along. And before I knew it, he had agreed to let me run for SGA office.

I told Mom as soon as I got home from school that I needed to start planning my campaign. She didn't look surprised. I don't think I have ever really surprised my mother by anything I've done. I think this is because we are so alike.

Mom and I were born on the same day. Well, not on the exact same day, obviously, because that would make us twin sisters! But we were both born on July 31. I like sharing my birthday—to a point. And then after that point, I don't like it, because *my* day turns into a day for *both* of us.

We also share a disease. Now that is a real bummer some people might say. As if

$$my\ life + disease = bad$$
$$and$$
$$my\ life + no\ disease = good.$$

I'm no math whiz, but really, it isn't that simple.

Mom always tells me that the world is very complicated, and that there are some things we just can't understand. That doesn't always mean that these things are terrible. It just means that you have to deal with them even if you can't figure them out.

My disease is very hard to understand. It's like muscular dystrophy, but not exactly. There's no big telethon or anything for it. We don't have posters on buses and we don't collect change at Halloween in little cardboard boxes. The name of my disease is even hard to pronounce: Charcot-Marie-Tooth. (You say that first word like this: Shar-ko.)

I know. What kind of name is that? That's what I thought when I first heard it.

Well, let me tell you, it has nothing to do with shark teeth. It is actually named after the three doctors who discovered it, like a hundred years ago. I figure you've got to be pretty full of yourself to name a disease after yourself. But maybe I'm wrong. Maybe if *I* discover something, I'll name it after myself: the Arlene Harper Condition. Hmm, catchy.

I just use the nickname for my disease—CMT—because it's certainly easier to say.

Both Mom and I have it. Well, we found out last year that she passed it on to me. My brother doesn't have it, and Dad doesn't have it, and no one throughout the entire known history of our family ever had it, until now.

This was the first—and the biggest—broken rule that I'd come face to face with. You're supposed to inherit CMT from someone who has it. But Mom got it from absolutely nowhere, and before she knew what it was, we found out I had it too. The doctors couldn't explain why no one else in our family passed it on to Mom. I heard one grown-up call it a "fluke." I have no idea what a fluke is, but I know I don't like it. It sounds like a vegetable.

So there we were last night, me and Mom, coloring my campaign posters. It was tricky, for sure. Having CMT means that my arms and legs don't always hear my brain talking to them. So my fingers are kind of weak, and my ankles are kind of wobbly. The braces help me to stand and walk and even run a little bit. Now, hills are a problem for me. Stairs I can do OK, but I feel better when I hold on to the railing.

As for my hands, well, if I'm playing Go Fish and I get stuck with a lot of cards, it's hard for me to hold all of them. But I can still write with a pencil. And I take piano lessons to help keep my fingers strong. I can play "Mary Had a Little Lamb" pretty good now.

On my campaign posters, Mom drew the letters and I colored them in. She held the marker between her two hands and moved her arms at the shoulders to make the long lines we needed. We wrote things like "Get on board with change! Arlene's your ticket!" and "Open doors for everyone! Vote for Arlene!"

Mom knows all about growing up with CMT because she has had it since she was little too. But she didn't know what it was until last year, when the doctors figured it all out. CMT gets worse as you get older, but it's different in each person. With some people, you might not even know they have it just by looking at them. With other people, you can tell right away—like with me and Mom. And I know it's sad, but some people even die from it. For most of us, though, CMT makes the muscles in our feet, hands, legs, and arms just get weaker and weaker.

So now Mom can't walk at all and uses a wheelchair to get around. Her hands and fingers don't move much anymore either, except for the pointer finger on her right hand, which she can lift high enough to tap her fingernail on the arm of her chair. But this is something I never want to see, because if she does this, it means she's really, really mad. When that finger starts tapping, you know you better clear out.

But Mom was nothing but proud of me today. She gave me a big good-luck kiss this morning at the bus stop. And now here I stood, with my face to the wind and posters in hand, ready to begin my political adventure.

TOUGH JOEY, SMART CARLOS

As I walked into the classroom, my teacher, Ms. Merrily, saw me struggling to hold on to all of my campaign posters with my stiff fingers. (No, I'm not kidding, her last name is really Merrily, and she is truly the most merry person I've ever met.) She greeted me with an "Oh my, Arlene, what have we here?" and came over to help.

"I'm running for SGA." I told her. "Secretary."

"Oh, darling, the rule is that only fifth and sixth graders can run for SGA. But I'm sure you'll make a wonderful SGA officer next year, honey." Ms. Merrily tilted her head as she talked, and her yellow hair reached down toward the floor, except right at the end near her shoulder, where it made a U-turn and bounced up into a cheery curl.

I tilted my head the other way, just for fun, so that if you put our heads together we'd make a head-X. "Well, I met with Mr. Musgrove yesterday, and he said it was OK for me to run. Apparently, the rule wasn't really a strict rule but more of a suggestion or something."

Ms. Merrily wobbled a little, as if something in her merry world was suddenly out of place, making her feel off balance. But she kept smiling and tilting her head, because otherwise she wouldn't be Ms. Merrily.

"You did? Really? Mr. Musgrove said that? Well, I'll talk with him myself, cutie-pie, just to make sure we all understand what the rules are. But let me put these posters over to the side of the classroom. My, aren't these wonderful! You must have worked really hard on these."

"Yup," I said, relieved to be free of those slippery posters. I walked over toward the little cubby room that was attached to our classroom to put away my backpack and coat.

It was crowded in there! Everyone was pushing and shoving, all trying at once to get their stuff hung up. I hesitated outside the door for a second, worried that I might get knocked down in that tornado of kids. I mean, even without a tornado I fall a lot. I've got so many scrapes and bruises, my knees look like they've been pecked by an army of ducks! Mostly it happens at home, but sometimes my legs just give way at school. I've learned to play it cool by pretending that I'm examining some ladybug crawling by or that I just feel like rolling in the grass. Sure, I laugh, but what I really want to do is scream, "Not again! Sufferin' sea serpents!" (It's Mom's favorite expression.) I'm hoping these leg braces help with all that falling.

While I waited for the cubby room to clear out, I watched Ketchup and Mustard, the class gerbils, wrestle in their cage, which sat on a shelf right outside the cubby room.

No, they aren't red and yellow gerbils. It was just that the class named them right after lunch on Hot Dog Day.

After a few minutes, the cubby room was still packed, but I decided to just dive in. Braces, shmaces—I can do everything that I always used to do.

I bumped and bounced like one of those wild Super Balls you get in goody bags at birthday parties. I eventually made it to the hook with my name label under it. I hung up my coat and backpack, threw my lunch into the lunch bucket, and got out my homework folder to take to my desk.

I turned around to find Joey Dangerfield standing in my path. He sure looked crumpled today, more than usual. His denim jacket was two sizes too big, and his pants flopped over untied sneakers. Bunches of brown hair spiked in different directions all around his head. Maybe he was up late. The Red Sox played last night, and they were still doing well. Dad says they usually don't mess up until just before the playoffs.

"Hey, Joey," I said, all friendly. He's one of the Tough Guys, and some kids were afraid to talk to him, but not me, not today.

"Hey, Arlene," he said. Then he raised his arm in the direction of my posters, which Ms. Merrily had rested against a shelf in the classroom. Just barely visible outside the edge of his huge sleeve was the end of a pointer finger. "What's with all those signs you got?"

"Oh, I'm running for SGA secretary. Want to vote for me?"

Joey stared at me for a second as his brain processed what I just said. Then bling! He understood. "No way! You're not allowed to run for SGA! That's only for fifth and sixth graders!"

I knew I had gone too far. Joey was never going vote for me. He always wanted to be in charge of things. I figured I'd better get out of this conversation quick.

"Well," I shrugged. "Mr. Musgrove said it was OK." Then I turned toward the cubby room door, but Joey kept talking.

"Well, jeez, *I* could be president!" Joey held his head high and put one hand over his heart, though I had no idea why. This wasn't the pledge of allegiance. This was the SGA.

"What? You're running for SGA?" It was Carlos, a Smarty. He probably wants to be president too, I thought. But probably because he could actually do the job, not just so he can control everything, like Joey wants to do. He looked like the opposite of the crumpled Joey. His brown pants were creased down the front, and tucked tightly into them was a yellow shirt with a collar. It looked like a church outfit.

"What do you care, Carlos?" Joey said. "You can't run anyway. No one would vote for you." Joey leaned toward Carlos, but Carlos didn't back away at all. He seemed lost in thought, like he didn't even notice this menacing Tough Guy. The thing about Carlos is that he's always thinking.

"I might run," said Carlos. "Yes, I could start small, with secretary or something, then work my way up the SGA ladder. Yes. Let me see. I would need a slogan." He pushed up his glasses, crossed his arms, and stared at the cubby room ceiling.

Joey gave up. He was getting no reaction from Carlos whatsoever.

Oh, this was terrible! If everyone else in the fourth grade runs for SGA, I thought, how can I possibly get enough votes to win? Being an SGA loser won't be impressive. I will become the Poor Girl with the Leg Braces Who Lost the Election.

"Who's running for SGA? Who would do that? We can't do that, can we?" Byron, one of my best friends, joined the conversation. Please, no more competition!

"I'm running for SGA secretary," I told the crowd that was now forming around me. I had to put an end to this. "All I know is Mr. Musgrove said it was OK if I ran in the election. I don't know about anyone else."

The kids then swarmed over to Ms. Merrily. "I want to run for SGA!" several of them shouted. "How come Arlene gets to and we don't?"

Ms. Merrily was now looking very off balance. I knew how she felt. But she managed to say in her singsongy voice, "Children! Everyone sit down now, please! I will speak to you about SGA only if everyone is sitting quietly in their seats!"

Kids scrambled to their desks. I almost got knocked down again. Sheesh, I really need some bumper guards on these braces!

"Now class," Ms. Merrily said, "there seems to be some confusion about SGA. I will talk to Mr. Musgrove and will let everyone know what the rules are. I'm sure it will all be cleared up right away. In the meantime, we have some things to do, my little learners! Now get going on your Morning Work, and we'll talk about this later."

We all picked up our pencils, but no one was actually working. Instead, whispers crackled throughout the classroom like static electricity. Everyone was talking about SGA. When the class was this noisy, kids sometimes had to flip their Behavior Cards. Everyone had a small booklet of cards that was tucked into a pocket on a big chart in the classroom. The booklets had green, yellow, and red cards in them. I heard Ms. Merrily tell other teachers that this was our "behavior system."

You see, Ms. Merrily didn't ever yell at anybody. Yelling would make her not so merry. If kids were misbehaving, she just told us cheerfully, "Flip your card!" as if this was something exciting, like there were prizes under the cards. But what it really meant was that now your booklet was open to the yellow card. If you flipped it one more time, to the *red* card, it meant you had to go see Mr. Musgrove.

While we were working and whispering, Ms. Merrily must have called Mr. Musgrove on that little phone/intercom thing that hung on the wall of our classroom, because after our Morning Work was over, Mr. Musgrove marched into our classroom. He stood tall in the front of the room, smoothed his tie, and buttoned his jacket. He nodded at Ms. Merrily, and she clapped her hands to get our attention. But we were already paying attention, because the principal was standing there!

"All right, students," he announced. "It has come to my attention that there is some confusion about the SGA election rules. Let me just clear it up for you. The rules state that only fifth and sixth graders can run for office in SGA. However, if there is a student in the fourth grade who is mature enough, responsible enough, and willing to do all that is required of an SGA officer, then it is within my power, as principal of this school, to allow that student to run for office. That person may very well be sitting right here in this classroom."

Kids all over the room looked at me and pointed. Some looked jealous (Joey!), but many had a look that said, "Wow!" My Big Plans were working. I was becoming that cool girl who ran for SGA in the fourth grade!

"And so," Mr. Musgrove went on, "I wanted to announce to you, and all of the fourth graders here at Greenwood, that if you wish to enter the SGA elections, you will need to follow the proper procedure. And that proper procedure begins with an essay, of no more than two hundred and fifty words, explaining why you are qualified to hold an SGA office. This is what all of the fifth and sixth graders have to do in order to participate in the election. I will read the essays submitted, talk with your teachers, and then I will determine on an individual basis whether it is appropriate for you to run for an SGA office."

Really? An essay? Now, I didn't know that. I was sure no one else knew about this either. I was betting that this would cut down on the number of kids who wanted to run for office.

"Does anyone have any questions?" Looking quite satisfied with his long, stretchy explanation of the rules, Mr. Musgrove slipped his hands into his pants pocket and rocked back and forth in his squeaky shoes.

Of course there were all sorts of questions. Anytime an adult asks us if there are any questions there are always thousands. Kids love to raise their hands and talk. This time most of the questions were not that important, though. They asked things like: Can we write in pencil? What if we write two hundred and fifty-*one* words—can we just take out a *the* somewhere? Do I need to put my signature on the bottom—because I don't know all my cursive letters yet? And so on.

As Mr. Musgrove answered the questions he kept taking little half steps toward the door, until he was basically standing outside the classroom with just his head sticking in the doorway. At that point, even though kids were still shouting out questions, he waved goodbye and took quick, clomping steps down the hall.

The class then turned their questions on Ms. Merrily, but she just sang out loudly, "Get your reading folders out, children! Rea—ding folders!"

I took out my folder, but my brain was already working furiously on that essay. Like Mom always says, if there is one thing I'm pretty good at, it's expressing myself.

MY CAMPAIGN COMMITTEE

At lunch, I made my way over to an empty seat next to Byron. He is my next-door neighbor and one of my best friends. He hates his name. He thinks it's weird. I love it because I can yell, "Bye-bye, Byron!"

"Arlene!" Byron shouted, even though I was sitting right next to him. "Arlene, how are you running for SGA? How do you get to do that? Huh, how? You talked to Mr. Musgrove? Arlene, you got guts!"

I shrugged and smiled. "I just made an appointment with him, and then he said that I could run."

"If you win SGA president, will you give me an extra hall pass that I can keep in my pocket? Will you get me extra pizza on Friday? Huh, Arlene, will you?"

"Byron, I don't think I can do that. Plus, I'm only running for secretary this year, not president." I stopped for a second and giggled. "I'll do president next year."

Byron thought about this, while lightly rubbing his fingers over his nearly shaved head. His parents believe in short haircuts. Frankly, if I were a boy, I'd choose a buzz cut like that too. My hair is thick and always tangled, and it hurts so much when Dad tries to comb through it.

We sipped from our mini milk cartons in silence for a minute, which was a record for Byron. He is a talker. That's another thing I love about him. You don't need to think about anything when you hang out with him. Byron just leads the way with all his chatter. Plus, he is short like me, and not that good at sports. He's more of a Smarty, like Carlos. So as two kids who like the idea of sports but are terrible at them, we are well-matched playmates.

I drank my usual chocolate milk, for extra energy. Byron slurped coffee milk. I have no idea how he can possibly drink that stuff, but Rhode Islanders sure love their coffee milk.

My other best friend, Lauren, came over. "Arlene, I can't believe you're going to try to run for SGA! How did you get Mr. Musgrove to let you do that?"

"I'm not sure, but I think he was feeling sorry for me."

"Why?" Lauren asked.

"People do that a lot. Mostly grown-ups."

Lauren stared at me with these big brown eyes that always remind me of warm cups of cocoa.

Maybe Lauren didn't realize some people might feel sorry for me now. She never really talked about my leg braces when she first saw them over the summer. I guess that's because she already knew me so well, and the braces were really no big deal to her.

Lauren grabbed my arm. "Well, then can I be your campaign manager, Arlene? I can help you hang your posters and figure out ways to get you votes."

"Me too, me too!" yelled Byron.

"Sure, guys, sure," I answered. "We'll all work together. But first I need to write my essay."

Just then Carlos slid down the bench of the long cafeteria table and bumped up against Byron. "Hey, Byron, you can't help Arlene! You have to help me. I'm running for secretary too. Come on, us guys have to stick together!"

29

Byron looked torn. He didn't have many friends other than me and Lauren, and now he had a chance to hang out with Carlos.

"Yeah," Lauren said as she flung her arm over my shoulder. "Arlene and I can manage just fine. Girls versus boys! This'll be great!"

Byron stared down at his milk carton, probably wishing he could get sucked in there like a genie going back into his bottle.

Carlos grabbed the sleeve of his shirt. "Look, Byron, come over here for a minute. I want to talk to you."

"Um, OK. I'll see you at recess, Arlene," Byron said.

"Yeah, Byron. Don't worry about anything." I gave him a little pat on the back. I figured I'd let him know later that there were no hard feelings.

As the boys got up to throw away their trash, I turned to Lauren. "Why is it girls versus boys? Doesn't that cut out half of my supporters?"

"Ah, don't worry about it, Arlene. I think there are more girls in this school than boys anyway. We just need to get the popular people on our side."

This worried me. I didn't hang out with popular people, like Jessie Fontaine, number-one Glamour Girl and most popular girl in the fourth grade, if not the whole school. With her good looks and great clothes, plus a bit of bossiness, she had a big group of girls following her wherever she went.

"We'll need to work on that, Lauren," I said.

At recess, my campaign manager and I got right to work. We approached the basketball court and called to the tallest girl there, Sheila McFadden, one of the best-known Sporty Girls. Her frizzy orange hair bounced wildly as she jogged over to us. "What's up, guys? I'm right in the middle of a game here."

Lauren leaned close to Sheila, her head just reaching Sheila's shoulder. "Listen, you know Arlene is running for SGA secretary, right?"

"Yeah. Way to go, Arlene." She swung her hand toward me and bopped me on my arm. I smiled and steadied myself.

"Did you also know that Carlos is running too?" Lauren asked. "He's getting all the boys to back him on his campaign. If you ask me, they're up to something, those boys. Us girls need to stick together."

"Well, I don't see what all this has to do with me," Sheila said slowly. "I'm not really that into politics."

Just as Sheila finished speaking, someone behind us shouted, "What do we have here, a little strategy huddle? You'll need it, girls, you'll need it, 'cuz there ain't no one that can beat our boy Carlos here!"

We turned around to find Joey Dangerfield with his arm around Carlos, who looked a little uncomfortable in the grip of this Tough Guy. Byron and a few other Smarties tagged along behind.

We girls were silent for a moment, taking in this unexpected scene. I found my voice first. "I thought you were running, Joey? For president, wasn't it?"

"Humph! I'm not writing some big essay!" Joey said. "Anyway, Carlos here is going to represent us boys in SGA. He'll be our man on the inside! We'll rule the school in no time! There'll be no more *taking turns* on the soccer field. It'll be whoever gets there first!"

The idea of the boys ruling the school *and* the soccer field didn't sit well with Sheila. She stepped up to Joey and Carlos, towering over them by several inches. "We'll just see about that, Dangerfield! My girl Arlene can beat your boy any day! And then a lot of things will change around here, like no more of you boys letting each other cut into the cafeteria line."

"Oh, yeah?" Joey let go of Carlos and stood up as tall as he could in front of Sheila. The two of them planted their feet and stared at each other through narrow eyes, like cowboys in an Old West showdown.

"Joey, let's go!" a voice called. "We got the soccer field! Come on!"

"This ain't over," Joey said through clenched teeth.

"No. It. Isn't." Sheila shot back.

The boys ran off, and Sheila turned toward us, grinning like a winner. "Oooh, this'll be fun!" she said. "Look, I gotta get back to my game, but we're going to do this. We can't back down now! Let me know how I can help!" And with a wave of her hand, Sheila jumped back onto the court.

"Lauren," I said, "I'm still not sure about making this into a boys-against-girls thing."

"It got Sheila on our side, didn't it? Come on, Arlene, we need to do everything we can to win. If you're in this, then you're in this all the way."

Pitting boys against girls didn't really feel like part of my Big Plans, but I couldn't back away now. That would not be very impressive! "You're right, Lauren. I'm in, 100 percent."

"Great. Next on our list: Jessie Fontaine."

Oh, man, I was hoping Lauren wasn't going to say that. Sheila and I always got along pretty well, even though we had nothing in common. Jessie was another story. She never talked to me, ever. I always felt like I was too short and too unimportant for her to be bothered with.

Lauren and I walked over to Jessie and her Glamour Girl friends, who were hanging on the monkey bars. Some of the girls were upside down; some were right side up. But when we got near them they all jumped to the ground and stared at us.

I sucked in a big breath and said, "Hey, Jessie, have you thought about the SGA elections? It looks like it's turning into a boy-versus-girl thing. I wondered if I could count on your support for secretary?"

Now that sounded quite political. Maybe I *can* do this.

Jessie pulled her long blonde hair back from her face and wrapped it in a fluffy pink ponytail band. She always wears one or two of these scrunchies around her wrist, along with some charm bracelets. Whenever she puts her hair into a scrunchie—or takes it out of one—you know Jessie has just made her point.

She glanced down her nose at me and shrugged. "I don't know. I don't really care that much about SGA, you know."

Jessie's friend Maddie chimed in, "*You* should run, Jessie! You'd win easily!"

"I know," said Jessie. "That's why I don't want to do it. What would be the point? Besides, who wants to write that big essay? Puh-lease. I could think of a lot better things to do with my time."

"Well," Lauren said, "if you're not interested in doing it yourself, wouldn't you rather see Arlene win instead of Carlos? And did you know that Joey Dangerfield is running Carlos' campaign? He says they're going to rule the school when Carlos wins."

"Rule the school?" Jessie said. "Yeah, right."

"Well, you certainly don't want to vote for them, do you?" I asked.

"No," Jessie replied. "But can *you* do the job?"

I was a little rattled by this question. What did she mean by asking that?

"Yes!" I said. "Yes, I can do the job."

Jessie pulled her scrunchie out of her hair and wrapped it around her wrist. "It requires a lot of *writing* you know."

It's true. I am a slow writer. But so what? I can manage. I stared at Jessie and then answered very slowly, "Yeah, I know."

"Just wanted to make sure," Jessie said. Then she shrugged and looked over at the field where the Tough Guys were playing soccer. "Yeah, whatever. I'll vote for you. Anything to keep the power out of the hands of Joey and his gang."

"Great!" Lauren said with a smile, like Jessie hadn't just flung an insult at me. "Thanks Jessie! We'll see you later!"

As we walked away, I turned to Lauren. "Didn't you hear what she said? *Do you think you can do all that writing?* I don't know if I even want her vote. She doesn't think I can do the job!"

"Oh, she was just talking, just being Jessie. Believe me, you do want her vote. All those other Glamour Girls will do what she does. That's a whole chunk of votes right there!"

"Yeah, but she's just voting for me because she doesn't want to vote for Carlos. It's like I'm the leftovers."

"Do you want to win or not? Prove her wrong, Arlene! Prove to her that you can do this."

Maybe Lauren was right. I did need Jessie's vote, and the votes of all her followers.

This election could be my own ticket to change. Winning might prove to everyone, even Jessie and Mr. Musgrove, that I can do anything I want to do, even if I have CMT.

38

SOMETHING TO PROVE

"Mom, can you read this over for me?"

I pushed my essay toward her. With the palm of her hand Mom moved the little knob on her wheelchair and drove into her space at the head of the kitchen table. She put her elbows on my paper to hold it in place.

I could hear Dad yelling at my brother Chris to clean up his room. Chris had become awfully messy since he turned thirteen. He had changed in a lot of ways after becoming a teenager, including turning into a giant overnight. From his view up there in the clouds, he suddenly thought everything I did was "for little kids." Yeah, well, I thought, when he has to call me Madam Secretary maybe he will change his tune.

I was hoping that Mom would like my essay. I made the usual points: I have good grades, I have just a few absences, and I'm a hard worker. I also pointed out that according to what we learned about government in social studies, a *democracy* means that all people have a chance to be part of the government. And the more people are involved, the better the government works. I even said that it is wrong to deny fourth graders the opportunity to run for office, just because somebody in charge thinks that fourth graders can't win. Who will be shut out next? Kids with disabilities? Short, unpopular people?

When Mom finished reading, she looked up with a big smile. "Wow, Arlene. Very strong essay. I'm really proud of you. It's a bold statement. And it must have taken a long time to write!"

"Yup it did. Thanks, Mom. I'm going to ask Chris to type it for me on the computer."

Dad came into the kitchen. "Don't ask Chris to do anything, Arlene. We'll help you. Your brother's got a lot of work of his own to do. Have you seen his room, Hon? It's a disaster."

"I know, I know," Mom said, shaking her head. "He's got to be more responsible."

"What are you reading?" Dad asked. He picked up my essay and must have done his speed-reading trick on it. Dad was an English teacher at the University of Rhode Island. He reads as quickly as a Labrador retriever in front of a bowl of dog biscuits. He looked up from my paper after just a few seconds and raised one eyebrow at me. "You're running for the Student Government Association, Arlene?"

Mom smiled and said to Dad, "She got special permission to run, Allan. She made an appointment with the principal and asked if she could run even though she's in the fourth grade, and technically only fifth and sixth graders are eligible to run. Can you believe it?" She looked at me, and I beamed right back at her.

Dad didn't join our Proud Party. He looked a little worried. "Are you sure you can do this, Arlene?"

I laughed. "Yeah, why, Dad?"

"I mean, it seems like a lot to sign up for right at the beginning of the year. Think about it. Can you run a campaign for SGA? And then, if you do win, can you handle being SGA secretary? We've got a packed schedule, you know, and the doctors said you'll probably feel more and more tired with all your therapy."

"It'll be fine. *I'll* be fine." I couldn't believe what I was hearing. First Mr. Musgrove, then Jessie Fontaine, now even my dad? Everyone was doubting me!

But unlike my other doubters, Dad really knows me. For a quick minute, I wondered whether he was right.

"I think she'll be OK," Mom said. "I think it's so great that she just went and asked for what she wanted. When I was her age, I never would have had the courage to do that. That's my girl." Mom touched her hand to my cheek.

"I just think she's jumping back into things way too fast," Dad said to Mom, like I wasn't even in the room. "What's most important here is that we do all we can to fight the effects of the CMT, not do all we can to be class president. I mean, come on. Where are our priorities?"

"It's secretary, Dad, but thanks for the vote of confidence."

Dad ignored my comment and waited for Mom to answer.

"I think we should talk about this later," Mom said, like she always does just when their conversations are getting interesting.

I wished I knew which things are OK for me to do and which aren't. But if Mom and Dad didn't even know the difference, then how could I?

I figured the only thing I could do was measure myself against my classmates. And they could all run for SGA if they wanted to.

This election was now officially huge—at least to me. I had a lot to prove.

BOYS V. GIRLS

The next morning I handed in my essay with high hopes. Ms. Merrily said she was going to send it along with any others to Mr. Musgrove for his review.

Just as we were getting started on our Morning Work, someone's mom came into our classroom. She whispered to Ms. Merrily, who nodded. Then Ms. Merrily stood up and said, "Class, let's have your attention up here, please. This is Mrs. Landers, the president of the PTA, and she would like to speak with you about a special opportunity."

"Hi guys!" Mrs. Landers began. She clapped her hands together and leaned toward us like we were her best friends and she was about to share a wonderful secret. "Listen, every year at this time the PTA has its membership drive, which is when we try to get as many people as possible to join the PTA. But this year we're doing something exciting. We're offering students a chance to be a PTA Membership Drive Spokesperson. For the next few days, you get to visit different classrooms in the morning to remind everyone to sign up for the PTA. It's a great chance to build your announcer skills! I'm wondering if anyone is interested in volunteering?"

Hands shot up all over the place. I thought about this for a minute and realized that it would be a great way for me to campaign for SGA. Students all over the school would get to know me. I raised my hand stiff and straight and as high as it would go.

"Oh goodness," Ms. Merrily said. "We have so many volunteers! My, my, my. OK, Mrs. Landers, how many children do you need?"

Mrs. Landers smiled weakly and said, "Oh, only two, Ms. Merrily, only two."

Ms. Merrily thought quickly. "OK, class, we'll have a lottery. Everyone who wants the job take a paper and write your name on it." Ms. Merrily

quickly handed out little pieces of paper to everyone. I wrote down my name, added a star and a heart
to it for good luck, and folded one corner down.
My brother taught me this trick for winning pick-
out-of-the-hat lotteries. Sometimes I like having an
older brother who knows these little secrets.

Ms. Merrily put all of the names into her New
England Patriots hat and swirled them with her
hand. Then she reached in and pulled out a name.

"Let's see," said Ms. Merrily as she unfolded the
first paper. "Maddie!"

"Yesss!" Maddie shouted as she jumped out of her
seat. When she looked around at everybody staring
at her, she covered her mouth and sank slowly back
into her seat.

Ms. Merrily swished her hand around in her hat
again. "And . . . Arlene!" she said.

I grinned and slapped my hand on my desk.
Good old Chris! I would have to thank him when
I got home.

"OK, Arlene and Maddie, you two are the PTA
Membership Drive Spokespeople," Ms. Merrily
said. "Come up here please so Mrs. Landers can give
you the information you'll need."

I walked to the front of the room and saw Mrs.
Landers' face kind of freeze when she saw my braces.
"Oh," she said to me, "Arlene, is it? Arlene, are you
sure you can do this?"

Mrs. Landers leaned toward me with a sweet but
worried smile. I wondered what in the world does
being a PTA Spokesperson have to do with wearing leg braces? But I leaned toward this lady and
just answered the question straight up. "Yes, Mrs.
Landers. Yes, I think I can."

Mrs. Landers looked a little embarrassed. I didn't
mean to make anyone feel bad, but I had to be honest. This PTA job was really my kind of thing. It had
politician written all over it.

"OK then, honey," Mrs. Landers said quickly,
"here is your information packet. It tells you what
rooms to report to each morning as school begins and
exactly what to say to each class. Good luck, girls!
Have fun with this, and sign up a lot of people!"

I returned to my seat with my new job assignment. Wow, PTA Membership Drive Spokesperson.
It was going to require extra time, but I had to do
it. It was the best way to campaign outside of my

grade. If I was going to run for SGA, I had to put in 100 percent effort.

Just before lunch, a student brought a note to Ms. Merrily. She announced, "Class, Mr. Musgrove has read your essays. He says, 'Good job to those students who have taken the time to meet the SGA election requirements. I am proud to announce that both of the fourth-grade students who wrote essays have been approved to run for SGA office. They are Carlos Martinez and Arlene Harper. Good luck to you both!' "

Ms. Merrily folded the note back up and looked up at all of us. "Well, that is just wonderful, you two. How lucky we are to have such dedicated students in our class! I know we will all give you our support in this important activity!"

Silent messages flew in many directions among the kids of Room 22. Joey's fist was clenched and raised slightly as he looked at Sheila. Sheila smirked and shook her head. She nodded confidently in my direction. I nodded back and glanced at Lauren, who beamed proudly. I smiled and rested my chin on my hands. It was on now. Let the race begin.

Out of the corner of my eye, though, I spotted an out-of-place frown. Jessie's forehead was wrinkled as she stared at me. Uh-oh, a crack in our solid girl network. I wondered if Jessie was rethinking her pledge of support.

At recess, I tried to get my mind off of Jessie. Lauren and I built a rock pile near the base of a big tree. We had found some beauties: smooth ones, sparkly ones, bright white ones. It was turning out to be an awesome collection.

Of course, that meant other kids wanted our rocks. Along came Spencer. He's one of the Scientists, those guys who love outer space, bugs, rocks, and anything slimy. He especially loves placing anything slimy in the nearest girl's backpack or desk, just so he and his buddies can have a big laugh. He once put a caterpillar on my shoulder! I didn't trust this guy, not at all.

He shuffled over to us. He was wearing his usual uniform, a glow-in-the-dark alien T-shirt. "Whatcha got there, Arlene?"

I knew he knew the answer, and I wondered what he was up to. I answered slowly, "A rock collection, Spencer. Why?"

"Just wondering," he said as he rubbed his hand through his hair. He bent down to inspect our treasure.

"It's ours," Lauren said quickly.

"I know!" Spencer shouted back at her. "I was just looking." He picked up the best rock, a perfectly smooth one with layers of glistening minerals in it. "Maybe I can just borrow this one. We need it for our alien game."

Lauren reached for the rock. "No, I don't think so. That's ours."

Spencer laughed and held the rock high above his head. "I'm just going to *borrow* it. I'll give it back. Later."

I joined in. "No way. Give it back right now."

"No," Spencer declared, like it was just that simple. He took a step back. "The playground is free land, and you can't claim any part of it as your own. So if I see a rock, I can take it. That's the rule. Ask Carlos. He's going to be our next SGA secretary anyway. Hey, Carlos!"

Lauren and I looked at each other. We had some fierce competition. Time to call for backup. "Sheila!" Lauren yelled toward the basketball court.

Sheila turned at the sound of her name and saw that it was Lauren calling. She made a time-out sign to the other kids on the court and jogged over. Carlos and some Smarties ran over too.

"What's going on here?" Sheila asked.

"Yeah, what is it Spence?" Carlos asked while folding his arms and bending his head toward Spencer.

"Look," Spencer explained. "This playground is for everyone to use, right? If I see a rock that I want to play with, I can take it, right? Just because some girls are standing near it, claiming that it's part of some *rock collection,* doesn't mean that they own the rock! Next thing you know, they'll say they own this tree, the whole playground, and all of nature!"

Sheila stepped up to Spencer and covered him in her shadow. "Listen up, you little alien creature, these girls said they're using this rock. So back off!"

"Who you tellin' to back off?" Joey said as he approached the growing crowd.

Sheila stepped away from Spencer and right up to Joey. "We're telling *you!*"

"You're not going to tell us anything," Joey said. "Our man Carlos here is going to set you straight. Just wait 'til this election happens. We're going to crush you, and then, when we're ruling the school, you girls won't have rocks or anything to play with!"

"Oh, yeah?" Sheila sneered. Then her hand shot out quickly toward Spencer. Like a basketball superstar swiping the ball on a fast break, she snatched the rock from him before he knew what was happening.

"Ah!" screamed Spencer. "Gimme that!"

Joey lunged for Sheila, but she easily stepped out of the way and ran toward the monkey bars. Joey raced after her, but he had no chance, really. Sheila is uncatchable. As the boys and girls began a humongous game of keep-away, the bell rang to end recess. This was good news to me. I might have a shot in the election, but there was no way I was going to help win a game of keep-away!

PTA POETRY

I was excited as I hiked my way up the steps of the bus the next morning. My PTA Membership Drive speech was tucked in my backpack, and I felt ready. I had practiced it five times in front of my mirror the night before.

The speech that Mrs. Landers gave me to read was not that interesting. Here's what it said: "Your family can join the PTA now! Fill out these forms and return them to school right away with your membership dues. It's a great way to get involved!"

I mean, that's fine if I was doing this for no reason. But I needed this spokesperson thing to get me votes. I had a lot riding on this election. So I jazzed up the speech a little.

I thought about all this as I rode along in the bus, staring out the window at these fields of nothing but green grass that went on and on as far as I could see. A lot of Rhode Island is just big patches of the same thing: grass, beach, shopping centers. I guess if you look at it quickly, Rhode Island might seem pretty dull. My relatives in New York tell me it is. But I think the people who live here, with all their little differences and customs, make it a pretty cool place.

We even have the longest state name: State of Rhode Island and Providence Plantations. That's our official name. Go ahead, look it up. The smallest state with the biggest name—weird, right? Like I said, we're only dull from the outside, at first glance. We have a lot of character up here.

Once I got to school, my first stop was a kindergarten classroom. "Attention, everyone," the teacher sang, "we have a visitor!"

I stood in the front of the room and looked out at all those little-kid faces. They seemed so young. I was like that too, so many years ago.

I hoped they liked my speech. I had turned the PTA announcement into a short poem, thinking it would sound better and make everybody laugh—and get the kids to vote for me.

I took a deep breath. I was going to do my best. That's all I could do.

"Hi everybody!" I said in my strongest voice, raising my hand to get their attention. "You ready?"

Then I started:

> *"So I'm here to say*
> *That it's time to pay*
> *For the PTA.*
> *No you can't delay*
> *'Cuz you knooowww*
> *They bring us shows*
> *That are sure to please.*
> *They buy us globes*
> *That we really need.*
> *And so we know*
> *How to reach our peeps*
> *They print up all of those*
> *Student directories."*

I clapped my two hands in the air above my head to try to get the crowd really into it.

"So come on everybody
Sign yourself up today
And I'll be on my way.
Don't wait another day
Join the PTA."

It was like someone pressed a big pause button. The room was silent. I must have shocked everyone. Maybe this wasn't such a good idea.

Then every kid started to clap, louder and louder. The teacher's smile broke her frozen face, and she clapped too.

"Is that what Mrs. Landers told you to say?" she asked.

"Not exactly," I said. "I changed it a little, just to make it kind of flow."

"Well, it was fantastic! Will you come back tomorrow?"

"Sure. See you later!"

Whew! Success! I walked happily out of that room, heading for the next one while thinking, Carlos won't be able to compete with this!

After a few more speeches, I went back to my classroom. Some kids were finishing their morning work, and others were reading in the Book Corner. I got my work done quickly and plopped down beside Lauren, who was sitting near the bookshelf.

"How'd it go, Arlene?" she asked. "Did everyone like your PTA speech?"

I nodded quickly. "Yeah! They all clapped, and the teachers were gushing, 'Oh, that was so good. Thank you, thank you!' I think this spokesperson job is going to really help in the election. Everyone will get to know me. I'm going to be, like, popular!"

I heard a snort behind me. Did someone leave a barn door open or something?

I turned to see Jessie sitting cross-legged behind me, flipping pages of a book without reading a thing.

"Did you say something?" I asked her.

"No."

I turned back to Lauren. "So anyway, I think this is going to be a really good thing."

"I'm just saying it takes more to be popular than some stupid PTA speech one morning out of your whole life," Jessie said.

I shuffled my body around on the floor to face Jessie. "Yeah, I'm not saying I'm going to be Miss Popular. I'm just saying that this is going to help in the election."

"Whatever," Jessie said with a shrug. Then she twisted her hair into a lime green scrunchie.

I pressed my lips together and turned to Lauren, who just shrugged. I knew I couldn't have Jessie against me. That would be awful for the election. So I tried to think of the best answer I could to her "whatever."

"Well," I said, "I just want to do what I can to win, so that Carlos doesn't. The only other person running for secretary is some fifth grader who just moved here. She probably doesn't stand a chance. It's up to us to keep Carlos out of the higher ranks of SGA."

"I guess," Jessie said. She smirked and shook her head. "You know, I probably should've run for office myself. That would have been the end of it. The girls would have rocked."

Thank goodness the candidate deadline was yesterday. The last thing I needed was to compete against Jessie!

Ms. Merrily called us all to come to Classroom Meeting time. I love this part of the week. We hear about things that are coming up, like assemblies and field trips; we learn about special projects that we'll be doing; and we discuss classroom "issues." They come from the notes that kids write and put in the Issue Box.

Ms. Merrily sat in her director's chair and crossed her legs neatly. We were all supposed to squash together on the rug in front of Ms. Merrily. They really needed to get a bigger rug, if you ask me. Since I was always the last one to make it to the rug, I had to fold my legs up in weird ways in order to get my whole self on there. Now with my braces, this was nearly impossible. I could have sat on the tile floor, but it was cold and dusty. I hated that. So today, I just kind of stood near the back of the crowd.

"OK, this is our third Classroom Meeting of the year," Ms Merrily said. "You've all done a wonderful job so far! You are my big fourth graders! But I want all of us to get to know each other even better, so I'm giving you a special assignment. It's going to be so much fun! I want each of you to bring in something from home, the most precious thing that you own. Then everyone will have a chance to tell the class about why their object is so special to them."

Carlos raised an index finger toward the ceiling and called out, "So you're talking about show and tell?"

"Well, Carlos, I call it Our Precious Things. We'll have one or two students present each day. I'll send home a paper that tells you on what day you should bring your Precious Thing to school."

"Can I bring in my video game?" Joey asked.

"No. I'm not talking about toys, dear, I'm talking about special objects, things that mean something to you. Maybe something you've received from a close relative, or an object that reminds you of a special event. Look around your house. Talk to your parents. See what you can find."

I needed to make a really powerful impression with this presentation. My most Precious Thing was going to say a lot about who I was, and this would either help or hurt me in the election. I had to give this major thought.

Ms. Merrily then announced that next week we would be going to the pumpkin patch for a field trip. Kids shouted out questions, high-fived each other, and just generally made a lot of noise.

"Settle down, boys and girls, settle down," Ms. Merrily said. "I'll also be sending home details about our field trip. Now, let's get to our Issue Box."

Everyone hushed up for this. It was so quiet we could even hear Ketchup chasing Mustard around their cage. Ms. Merrily reached inside the box and pulled out the first issue.

She read aloud, "The girls stole a rock right out of a kid's hand. They should get in big trouble."

Kids giggled behind cupped hands. Ms. Merrily shook her head quickly. "No, this is not OK, not at all. First of all, the Issue Box is not the Blame Box. Tattling on each other is not appropriate. And second, this makes me sad to think that there is any stealing going on in my class. We are all friends, aren't we? What happened to 'Room 22 sticks together like glue'? No more taking what isn't ours, friends! I trust that this issue is put to rest!"

I looked around at the kids of Room 22. Sheila smirked proudly. Joey grinned wickedly. Spencer's cheeks were spotted red. No, this issue was not resting at all. In fact, it was actually just about to wake up, and with a fierce roar.

SURPRISE ATTACK

At recess, Lauren and I abandoned our rock pile. I felt it was best for the campaign. And besides, Lauren wanted to practice her flips on the monkey bars.

I never play on the monkey bars, obviously. So I wandered around the blacktop, until a basketball rolled to my feet.

"Hey Arlene! Throw it over here!" Sheila called.

Sheila and a few other Sporty Girls were playing basketball. I picked up the ball and pushed it into the air toward the court. It bounced three times before it reached Sheila.

"Thanks, Arlene!" Sheila said. "Want to play?"

Well, this was different. The Sporty Girls were inviting me to play with them! This never happened before. Even before I got my braces, the CMT was still in my body. I'm just awful at anything athletic. Nobody ever asked me to play any kind of sports.

I knew I was going to stink at this, but I really wanted to try. I did my best. It was all I could do. But the leg braces didn't make an athlete out of me. After a while, Sheila looked like she was sorry she had asked me to play, especially on her team. But she was nice about it. She just passed the ball to other people, and I ran around, trying not to interfere with the actual players.

All of a sudden our game was interrupted by a big "Aaaarrrrgggghhhh!"

Out of nowhere came a herd of boys. The Tough Guys, the Smarties, even some of the Scientists were there. And they were carrying armfuls of leaves.

They charged the court and threw all these crinkly brown leaves on the Sporty Girls' heads, and on my head. I managed to stay on my feet, but barely.

The girls screamed. The boys shouted, "We rule!" and ran away. It was your classic run-by attack, used by boys throughout playground history.

"You're going to get it!" Sheila screeched at the boys. "You are *in for it*!"

She tried to untangle twigs from her mop of frizzy hair. She noticed me and came over. "Are you OK, Arlene?"

"Yeah, I'm fine," I said, laughing.

Sheila screamed in the direction of our enemies. "You nearly knocked Arlene down and *killed* her, you big bullies!"

"No, really, I'm fine," I told her.

"I'm trying to make a point, Arlene."

Lauren ran up to us. "Whoa, what happened?"

"It was wild!" I said. "The boys just attacked us! So crazy!" I brushed off my jacket but couldn't wipe the wide grin off my face.

"It's on now," Sheila said slowly, staring off toward the field. "Oh, it's on now. Come on, girls. Emergency meeting. Hey, Maddie, Jessie, we've got revenge to plan!" Sheila and the other Sporty Girls took off in the direction of Jessie and her friends.

I stayed on the basketball court while Lauren helped me pull off the bits of leaves stuck on my clothes. Where are those recess aides when you need them? They were all over us when we were picking all the pretty flowers last spring. Now they were nowhere to be found.

"Arlene, I don't know about this," Lauren said. "Like you said, it's getting a little crazy."

"What? Are you kidding me? I'm back, Lauren! I never felt better in my life!"

I hadn't told Lauren about my Big Plans. She probably didn't even realize that people might look at me differently this year because, well, she didn't. So she also probably didn't understand how great I felt after I got leaves dumped on my head by a bunch of wild boys. Knowing Lauren, she probably just felt worried.

But it all made perfect sense to me. At this moment, I wasn't different any more. With twigs in my hair and leaves tickling my neck, I was one step closer to being just like everybody else.

QUEEN TATTLETALE

That night at dinner, I bit happily into my grinder.

OK, for all you non-Rhode Islanders, a grinder is what you probably call a "sub," those long sandwiches stuffed with sliced meat, cheese, pickles, and a whole bunch of other stuff that they throw in there. I know, *grinder* doesn't make much sense. But I guess a sandwich has as much to do with a grinder as it has to do with a submarine, a subway, or a substitute teacher.

We got dinner on our way home from my physical therapy session. We always do takeout on these nights because Dad has to race to pick up Mom at the school where she works as a speech and language therapist, then race to my aftercare to get me, then drive all the way up to Warwick where my session is. By the time we get home to South County, we have to eat a quick, take-out dinner so that I can get my homework done before bed.

"How was school today, Arlene?" Mom asked.

"Exciting!"

"Wow. You learned great things?"

"No. But recess was a blast!"

"That was always my favorite period, too," Chris said from his slouch. "Just wait, squirt. When you get to middle school, like me, there's no more recess."

Yeah, yeah, yeah. He's older than me, knows more than me, is always five steps ahead of me. I got it. I didn't need to hear it again.

"Anyway," I continued. "During recess I got stuck in the middle of a ferocious battle!" I figured Mom would love this: her brave girl, off to war!

Mom swallowed hard. "Wow. Are you OK?"

"Yeah. It wasn't like a dangerous battle. But the boys charged us girls on the basketball court and threw big bunches of leaves on us. It was wild!"

"What?" Dad said. "Where were the recess aides?"

"Who knows? But no one got hurt or anything. It just made this election even more exciting!"

"How is attacking girls with leaves part of a student election?" Dad demanded.

"Well, see," I explained, "my main competition is Carlos. All the boys are supporting him, and all the girls are supporting me. So it's kind of turning into this big war!" I spread my arms out wide to help Mom and Dad understand how big, and how exciting, this was.

Chris sat up. "You should have thrown leaves back on them!"

"No! No, she shouldn't!" Dad objected.

"Arlene," Mom said, "I don't like the sound of this at all. Someone could have gotten hurt. I'm going to e-mail Ms. Merrily." Mom's forehead got that little worry wrinkle in the middle.

"Mom, Please don't! Please! I don't want to be a big tattletale. Nothing bad is going to happen."

"Mom is right, Arlene," Dad said sternly. "I told you that you were taking on too much too quickly. You need to just slow yourself down."

"Come on! I'm just doing what everyone else is doing. I'm sure no one else's mom is going to e-mail the teacher over some leaves! I'll look like a dork! I'll lose the election!"

Mom shook her head, wrinkle and all, and studied me. I hoped she was thinking about how no one would vote Queen Tattletale for secretary.

I held my breath. Mom breathed out a sigh. "Let's just eat," she said. "We'll talk about this later."

Later came all too quickly. After dinner I was sitting on the floor of my room, flipping through my humongous book about horses, when Mom rolled in. She looked serious. I stood up to meet her face to face.

"Arlene, listen. I'm glad that you're off to a great start this year. But I'm not going to sit by and watch you or somebody else get hurt. If anything like this happens again, I'm going to e-mail your teacher."

"Fine." I flopped on my bed and squished a pillow under my chin. "I won't let it happen again. Because if you end up e-mailing Ms. Merrily, I'll look like some wimpy kid in leg braces!"

Mom moved closer to me. "What in the world does any of this have to do with your leg braces? Arlene, student elections don't involve fighting with boys, period. I don't care if you wear braces, you use a wheelchair, or you've got no legs at all! It's just not right."

"But, Mom . . ."

"Arlene, you know this isn't right. I'm not saying you can't continue running for secretary. I'm saying you can't take part in some crazy boy-girl war."

I looked down and noticed Mom's finger hovering in the air above the arm of her wheelchair. It was about to start tapping.

Yeah, I was going to get nowhere in this argument.

I figured I'd better switch strategies quickly and try to lighten up the atmosphere. "But didn't you say you named me Arlene because it means courage? I'm a courageous soldier now. You can't take me away from the front lines just when the action is starting!" I slid off my bed and saluted Mom, with a serious soldier frown on my face, waiting for her to crack a smile.

I had to wait a long minute, but it worked. Mom's finger lowered, along with her shoulders, and the faintest smile appeared. She shook her head. "Put your hand down, you crazy girl." I lowered my arm and leaned against Mom's chair. "But let me ask you something," she said. "Why did you say you'll look like a wimpy kid?"

"Because everyone else is all into this war thing. The girls are already planning their next move. If I don't go along, they'll think I can't handle it."

"Do you believe that? That's how you think people look at you?" Mom looked at her lap and then up to the poster of a famous painting that's hanging on my wall. "Honey, look at that picture there."

When you hold your face right up to the poster, it looks like a bunch of colorful little splotches. But when you back away, you see a pretty bridge over a lake and all these flowers and stuff.

"This is one of my favorite paintings," Mom said. "It was done by an artist named Claude Monet. I love the way you can see almost all of the paint strokes. You can really see the way the different individual parts make up a beautiful whole."

"Yeah, it's really cool, Mom." I always liked the poster, but how come we were suddenly talking about art?

"People are like that, Arlene. There are the individual parts of us, which are very important. And then there's the big, beautiful picture. I mean, sure, you and I have CMT, but that's not the only thing there is to know about us."

Her voice was really kind and soft now. "You are truly my courageous girl, but you're also very smart, and you know what's right and what's not. Some crazy boy-girl war or even this student election has nothing to do with your courage or your abilities."

"OK," I mumbled.

Mom leaned over to give me a hug. I draped my arms around her neck and squeezed her back. I sure do love my mom, but right then I totally disagreed with her.

This election had everything to do with everything. It was my chance to prove that I'm just like everyone else, that CMT can't hold me back.

Anyway, it was too late. I was already involved. I was a budding celebrity from my PTA gig. I had a good shot at winning the election.

And if there was going to be a war, I wanted in on it.

FROM NERD TO NINJA

The next morning at school, I walked down the hall to the bubbler to get a drink. Rhode Islanders called their drinking fountains bubblers. Well, the water kind of bubbles up, doesn't it?

Of course, in Rhode Island, it's pronounced bubblah because, according to Mom, the speech therapist, Rhode Islanders often don't say their R sounds, especially at the ends of words. She cured my father of this speech problem when she first met him, and she stomped it out of Chris and me before it ever got going. Mom's on many missions, including a crusade to fix the way Rhode Islanders talk, one person at a time.

Like I said, it's different up here. We make up our own words and then pronounce them in our own way. It keeps the out-of-towners guessing.

The air was tingling back in Room 22. The boys knew that the girls would strike back, but they didn't know where or when. They watched us like they were security guards in a diamond shop.

It was so exciting! We were undercover agents. Sheila scribbled something on a scrap of paper, crumpled it up, and threw it on my desk. "We talk during math," the note said. "Those boys are done!" She jerked her head to the side. I understood her signal that I was supposed to pass the note on.

Secret messages, signals, and plans—and I was a major part of all this. Arlene was back on the scene!

Later, during snack time, I was eating my chips and talking with Byron.

"Have you written your campaign speech yet, Arlene, huh? What're you going to say? Is it going to be funny? Are you nervous?"

Sometimes I wish Byron didn't always ask four questions at once. I never know which one to answer. This time I picked one in the middle.

"No," I said, "it's not going to be funny. It's going to be real."

He chewed on that for a minute.

"Real what?" he asked.

"Never mind," I said. "What's going on with you? Are you on Carlos' side or what? I don't really like how we're all splitting up over this."

"I don't like it either," Byron said, lowering his voice. "You're my best friend, Arlene, but if I don't back up Carlos, I'll never be one of the guys!"

"Well, what did you tell Carlos the other day in the cafeteria?"

"I told him I'd think about it."

"Good move."

"Hey, Brian," a voice behind us called. "You with us or what?"

Byron and I looked in the direction of the voice. It was Joey. Carlos stood behind him, watching Byron eagerly.

Byron stood up to meet the boys face to face. "First of all," he said, "my name is Byron, not Brian."

Then Byron folded his arms and stood up even straighter. You tell 'em, my friend! I thought.

"And second of all," he continued, "yep, I'm in." He slapped the hands of his fellow soldiers, and then all sorts of slapping, shoving, and grunting followed. I turned away.

Byron returned to his seat next to me when it was over. He looked down, trying to hide his smile.

"What do you think you're doing?" I asked. "I thought you couldn't decide who to support in this election."

"I know," he said, "but they never include me in anything. And now they want me on their team! Will you be mad at me if I say I'm with them, huh? I don't want you to be mad at me. But can you believe it? I'm one of the guys!" He pounded his chest like some big gorilla. Then he scrunched his face in pain, because either he punched harder than he thought, or his chest was more sensitive than your average gorilla's. He leaned forward and tried to rub the sore spot without me noticing.

I grinned. I certainly understood. Sometimes, you've got to push yourself, "expand your horizons" as Mom says. "I'm not mad at you, Byron. Just make sure you still vote for me."

Byron looked first to one side, then to the other, and then behind him. When he was sure that nobody was eavesdropping on our conversation, he leaned over to me and whispered, "Don't worry. You got my vote."

The intrigue just kept getting thicker.

When I got back to class, it was time for the Precious Things presentations. Carlos was up first. Good. I would get a chance to check out how this Smarty used his time in front of the class to earn more votes. I got ready for a talk about some big book he just finished reading, or some detailed model ship that he just built, to prove how smart and capable he was.

Carlos walked proudly to the front of the room. He pushed his glasses closer to his eyes and cleared his throat. Then he held up a long, dark green sash that stretched from his raised hand all the way to the floor.

"This is my newest sash that I got from kung fu," said Carlos. "I'm in my third year, and I finally reached the level where I get to use a broad sword. I couldn't bring the sword into the classroom because it's not safe. Sifu, which means teacher in kung fu language, taught us that swords aren't toys, that they are serious weapons, and they should only be used in a safe manner in the kung fu classroom or in a big practice space at home. It's part of the respect for kung fu that any martial artist has to have."

Joey raised his hand. "Wait a minute. You telling me that all this time I've known you, you've been, like, a kung fu master?"

"No, not a master yet," said Carlos. "Only Sifu is a master. But I'm on my way. I know lots of different kicks and punches, and I can use a long pole to fight. Right now I'm learning how to use the sword. I'm going to be like Jet Li and Jackie Chan."

The class was hushed. No one could believe that this nerdy-looking kid was actually a kung fu fighter.

Ms. Merrily broke the silence. "Can you tell us why this object is so special to you, Carlos?"

"Well," said Carlos with a small grin, as he wrapped his big sash around his waist, twice. "Kung fu is something that nobody here knew about me, until now. It was my secret weapon—all this time.

It has made me powerful and strong. Now, with the elections coming up, I felt it was the perfect time to reveal my secret."

He puffed out his chest and stood stiff and tall like a bronze statue, with his fists clenched by his sides. "I'm now very proud to show all of you my raw toughness."

We admired his raw toughness as he walked through the aisle with his sash around his waist and a don't-mess-with-Carlos attitude. Joey, with his mouth forming an O and his eyebrows raised high, lifted his hand for Carlos to slap as he went by. As Carlos sat down, Spencer knocked clenched fists with him.

It looked like I had some stiff competition here. I would just have to work even harder. I can do this, I thought. I know I can. But I needed to really step up my campaign to top Carlos.

Later, in math, it was time for group work. This basically meant chat time. The girls and I sat in groups of four, with our knees on our chairs and our butts in the air, and we all leaned on our elbows toward the center of the square that our desks made. This day we all had our heads together, looking at a sheet of word problems. (No wonder we have a lice problem at school. I put my hands on my skull as a shield, just in case.) While we aimed our eyes at the math problems, we talked campaign strategy.

"Carlos did a really good presentation today," Lauren said. "He totally changed his image from nerd to ninja!"

"He sure did," Sheila agreed.

"Well," I said, "what's my image right now?"

Jessie looked my way. "You really want to know?"

I sat up straight. "Yeah!"

Lauren waved her hands to tell me to kneel back down. "No, listen," she whispered. "Arlene has a great image. She's getting to know so many kids through the PTA thing. We're fine. We've got to stick with our plan, just get Arlene out there to as many students as possible, especially outside the fourth grade. That's where we have an advantage over Carlos."

Jessie slapped her palm on the desk, startling me. "I don't think we can take any chances here," she said. "If the boys win, we'll all be doomed. I should have entered the race myself. I can see that now. But we can't just *stick with our plan*. We need to act and get back at those boys in a way that crushes them."

"I totally agree!" Sheila said. "Those boys need to pay, especially after what they did to us at recess. If we top them and their little leaf attack, we'll have the advantage again. Everyone start thinking!"

I sat back in my seat, wondering what Jessie would have said about my image if Lauren had let her answer. Maybe I didn't want to know.

A MELLOW CELLO

"How is the PTA Membership Drive going?" Dad asked. We were having one of my favorite dinners: elbow macaroni and meatballs. I like all kinds of pasta *except* spaghetti, because spaghetti is way too hard for me to twirl on a fork.

I was happy to talk about something other than the election, and the war brewing behind it, because I didn't want to get a big lecture again. "It's great, Dad! I've been making up my own rhymes to say instead of the speech that Mrs. Landers gave me."

"Are you allowed to do that?" Mom asked.

"Um, I don't know. Why not? I mean, everyone likes it, even the teachers."

"Do you always just do things your own way?"
With the fork that was woven in between several of
her stiff fingers, Mom drew little circles in the air
between us. She was trying to joke around and look
as if she was really mad, but she was smiling a big,
proud smile.

"Yup," I said. "I'm telling you, it's much better.
And I think I'm going to change the style too. I've
been doing rhymes, but maybe tomorrow I'll do
something really different, like an original song."

"Original song!" Chris said. "You're crazy." He
had to get in with his opinion.

"Have you ever been a PTA Membership Drive
Spokesperson?" I asked Chris. But I didn't wait for
his answer, because I knew it was no. "Then you
don't know what you're talking about."

"I know that you can't write the words and the
music to an original song all in one night. And I know
that you can't have, like, some kind of band in the
classroom to play the music for you. So I think I do
know that an original song is pretty impossible."

Well, he had a point. But I would never admit
that. Never!

"You don't know diddly," I said.

"Arlene, I'm sure you will do great!" Mom said. "You do whatever you want. Be creative. You're very good at that!"

"Yeah, Chris, support your sister," Dad said, popping Chris on the back of the head with his palm.

"OK, fine. Arlene, do your song. Here, I'll even help you." Chris stood up, put his hand on his chest, and began singing at the top of his lungs. "Ohhh, join the PTAaaaaay. If you want me to stop singing, you must paaaayyyyy!"

Dad threw his napkin at Chris, which he needed because he forgot to swallow his food before he began singing, and tomato sauce was now dripping down his chin. Mom rolled her eyes and looked at me. It was our usual secret girls' look, the one that says we're two souls lost in this crazy family, this world full of people who can never understand what it's like to be us. It's the most comforting look in the world.

Except that now I worried about what Mom would say if she knew that I was still involved in the whole war thing. Suddenly, I felt all alone, like I was wandering far away from my family in some dark forest, like I was Gretel without Hansel, or any breadcrumbs.

But I stuffed that feeling back down, deep inside of me. If I didn't think about Mom's reaction, this whole thing was totally thrilling. When I came back to school this year, I was just the poor Girl with the Leg Braces. Now I was Arlene on the Scene, mixed up in a crazy race of revenge and political plotting. Stay tuned for the next exciting episode!

The next morning, the sun found little Rhode Island and shone brightly as I worked my way down the bus steps. I was feeling great today. I had my new Membership Drive speech prepared, and I was hoping it would boost my campaign even more. After his strong presentation yesterday, everyone was talking about the "new Carlos."

In a first-grade room, I launched into my song (to the tune of "Three Blind Mice"):

"Three more days.
Three more days.
Join the PTA.
Join the PTA.
So sign up now to join our team.
And make this school the best it can be.

Together we'll all learn happily.
We are family.
It takes you and me."

OK, it wasn't completely original, but I did come up with the words. And the kids clapped and clapped. I took a slight bow because it just felt right. The teacher gave me a little hug and told me to please come back tomorrow.

This PTA spokesperson gig was terrific. So many people were getting to know me. It really was going to help in the battle against the ever-popular Kung Fu Carlos.

Later, as we all finished our snacks, Ms. Merrily told us to clean up for more Precious Things presentations. We scrambled to get ready. Crumbs flew off desks, little plastic bags floated gently to the floor in the general area of the trash cans, and juice boxes dripped red, spotty trails down the aisles. Someone threw leftover carrots into Ketchup and Mustard's cage. Soon we were ready to listen.

Sheila was up next. I figured she would have a team jersey, a football, or a trophy.

She clomped with long steps in high-top basketball sneakers to Ms. Merrily's closet at the front of the room. She removed a tremendous black bag, unzipped it, and took out what looked like a violin made for the Jolly Green Giant.

"This is my cello," Sheila began. "I'm learning to play. I've been taking lessons for a whole year. A lot of kids can't play a cello because it's too big, but I'm tall and strong, and it's no problem for me. Watch."

Sheila sat down in a chair and put this gigantic instrument between her legs. She then slid a long stick along the strings of the cello. The stick was like the thing that comes with a violin, except this one was as long as a baseball bat.

The sound came out squeaky at first then made a low moan, like a whale. But eventually the notes became clear, sort of. I thought I heard "Old McDonald" in there somewhere. Sheila had her eyes closed as she pulled the stick across the strings, and her head was tilted slightly to the left. It looked like the music was really moving her.

When she finished, she raised her head. She looked all refreshed, like she just drank a glass of lemonade. Then she stood up, held the arm of the cello with one hand, and took a deep bow, flipping the stick up into the air with her other hand.

There was a moment of shocked silence as she did this, but then we all clapped.

Sheila finished her bow. "Thank you, thank you," she said. "My cello teacher says that if I practice every day, I can play grown-up, classical songs by a guy named Mozart and some other dude named Bach. Someday I could even play in an orchestra. I never knew it, but I have music in me!" She puffed out her stomach and chest, like the music was going to pop out, right then and there.

Wow, this was really cool. Who would have thought this Sporty Girl had music in her? And not, like, rock 'n' roll, but grown-up music, played on this humongous violin.

Kids had all sorts of questions. How much did the cello weigh? How much did it cost? What was her teacher's name? Did the cello fit under her bed?

I just smiled. I liked Sheila even more after her presentation. She was always nice to me, and she's also fun and unpredictable. But I was going to find out even more about her adventurous side tomorrow at the pumpkin patch.

PLUMPY THE
STEAMROLLER PUMPKIN

I bounced in a backseat on the bus as it rattled down Route 1 toward the pumpkin patch. Thank goodness I was safely squished between Lauren and Byron because there was no way I could have held on if I was next to the aisle or the window, which would have been hazardous to my head.

The mood on the bus was pretty intense. Everyone was pumped up for the pumpkin patch, but kids were still wrapped up in the whole war thing too. So it was like this: Let's say you take a cup of the feeling you get right before your birthday party starts. You pour that into a bowl and mix it with a cup and a half of the feeling you get just as you and your brother begin tackling each other. Then you stir it up, 'til it's bubbly and foaming, and pour it over fifty fourth graders squashed into a school bus bumping down a dirt road toward a pumpkin patch. And *that* was what we were dealing with.

Carlos was standing up, hanging on to his own seatback and the back of the seat in front of his. He leaned against the open window, and the wind scattered his hair all around his head. He cracked jokes with Joey, compared alien knowledge with Spencer, and even teased Maddie about her new haircut. This guy had suddenly transformed from the Thinker into Mr. Popularity.

"I'm in trouble," I muttered to Lauren.

"Yeah," Lauren nodded as she stared at Carlos.

"Hey! You're supposed to be my campaign manager!"

Lauren shook her head quickly, as if she were trying to break some kind of spell that Carlos had put on her. "I am! But a good campaign manager doesn't lie to her candidate. She keeps it real. And we're in real trouble."

"Thanks."

"But we're not going to give up! We've got to step it up!" Lauren pumped her fist in the air.

"Hey, nice slogan," I said. "You're right. We can do this. We have to do this. We'll just step it up."

"That's the attitude! You've got one more PTA speech, right? And a week more of campaigning. Oh, and your Precious Things presentation. Come on, it's not over yet!"

"Yeah, that's true."

The bus pulled into a grass parking lot and slowed to a squeaky stop. Kids streamed down the bus steps, and I just sort of rode the surf of this wave, because really, it was that or be trampled.

Once on solid ground, I looked out at Plumpy Pumpkin Farms. The parking lot was really a large, open field, with yellowish green grass and surrounded by splashy-colored trees.

But this pretty landscape was interrupted by . . . who else but Plumpy the Pumpkin. Plumpy was a big ole balloon pumpkin, like those huge moon bounces you find at fairs. This orange monster sat proudly on top of a very steep hill beyond the trees, welcoming all to Plumpy Pumpkin Farms. You know, in case you forgot where you were.

Plumpy had a little orange tail connected to a pump that kept him full of air. He was held in place with thick ropes looped around stakes in the ground. He swayed slowly in the cold breeze and wore a big, black, toothy smile. I could almost see a little twinkle in his eye. If he were a kid, I would have guessed that he was up to something, that Plumpy.

Ms. Merrily had recruited some parents to chaperone us on this field trip, and she was trying to get them organized so that they could organize us kids. But everyone was just running around near the buses, having just sat still for thirty minutes (well, kind of still, if you didn't count all that bouncing and switching seats).

We finally got moving toward some wagons attached to tractors. These tractors were going to take us to the actual pumpkin patch. Apparently, we had been running around the pumpkin patch lobby.

The chaperones called this little tractor adventure a hayride. But these wagons looked pretty rickety. How was I supposed to hang on with my stiff fingers and weak knees as we lurched back and forth? I love to roll in the hay as much as the next kid, but these wagons needed some kind of safety belts back there.

I watched everyone clamber on board. Well, I could either admit I couldn't ride in the back like everyone else, or I could figure out some way to do it.

Lauren reached out her hand. "Come on, Arlene! Get in!"

Ah, forget it! I can do anything that I want to, anything that everyone else does. I heaved myself into the wagon and held on the best I could.

We bumped out toward the pumpkin fields. We rode along a well-beaten path through trees dotted with worn decorations that the farmers must have put up years ago. There were wooden cutouts of Bugs Bunny and Mickey Mouse dressed as ghosts. A tattered witch swung on a broom tied to a high tree branch. A sign read "Keep Out! Spooky Pumpkins on the Loose!"

Right on cue, everyone screamed at these signs and signals because it was all just part of the fun. But I was having no fun at all. I was barely hanging on. As we crossed a small stream, the tractor leaned way to the right, and the wagon tipped sharply to the left. Kids shouted with glee. I grabbed Lauren's hood in horror. I was about to fall out of this crazy thing and into the muddy stream!

"Ow, you're choking me!" Lauren snapped, and she grabbed my hands to yank them off of her hood.

"Hold on to me, Lauren!" I said. "Hold on! There's about to be a girl overboard!"

Lauren giggled and held my hands. She seemed to find the whole situation amusing. I played it off like, sure, wasn't this funny? I was about to fall off of a wagon, splash into muddy water, and probably get run over by a tractor. Good times, good times.

I was so relieved when we finally arrived at the rows of pumpkin vines. I just stood still for a few minutes, with my feet planted firmly on solid ground again. Then I took my time looking for the perfect pumpkin, being careful of all those twisty, trippy vines.

I found a nice round one, with good orange color, one that I thought would make a terrific jack-o'-lantern. Kids were running all around the vines, trying to find the biggest pumpkin that they could lift. Byron picked a tall and narrow one so he could make a ghost out of it. Spencer chose a bumpy gourd to make a Halloween alien. Eventually all the kids returned to the tractors with their treasures and got them marked with their initials in permanent markers.

As I struggled to get back onto the Wagon Death Trap while carrying my pumpkin, the guy who was driving the tractor came over to help. He looked just like I pictured a farmer would look: baggy jeans, big boots, and a thick flannel jacket. But instead of a straw hat, he wore a Pawtucket Red Sox cap, and he had it pulled down so it almost covered his eyes.

The guy lifted his hat slightly and looked me up and down, stopping for a long minute at my leg braces. "You going to be OK back the-ah? Maybe you should ride up front."

I looked at all of the other kids gathered happily in the wagon. But then I thought of the path back to the main area, back across that dangerous stream.

"Yeah," I said loudly enough for most of the kids to hear, "now with all the kids *and* the pumpkins back here, there's not enough room for me. Maybe I should ride up front with you."

"Show-uh," Farmer Paw Sox said, and he helped me climb up onto the wide tractor seat.

Joey yelled from the wagon, "Hey, I thought no kids up front! That's against the rules."

I just smiled. Welcome to my world, Tough Guy.

Farmer Paw Sox and I got to know each other a little on the way back from the pumpkin patch. He was a really cool guy. I never would have guessed it by looking at him, but he wasn't really a farmer at heart. He was just working here at his uncle's farm while he tried to become a rock star. I told him I'd look around town for his band, Chicken Coop Riot. Well, when I got old enough to go to rock concerts I would.

My new rocker friend was born in Rhode Island, which I had guessed by his accent. Not only do Rhode Islanders ignore Rs in most words, according to Mom, but they also throw R sounds into words where they have no business being.

"I had no idea-r that it might be hahd fo' you back in the wagon," he said to me. "Sorry 'bout that."

"It's no problem," I said. "I mean, you couldn't think of every little thing when you set up this pumpkin patch deal. Believe me, this happens all the time. I just figure things out."

"Yaw one tough cookie, I bet."

"Yep, that's me. It just means that I have to bend the rules sometimes to make things work for me. No big deal."

Farmer Paw Sox smiled and pulled his cap back down over his eyes. He seemed to want to think about this for a while.

I leaned against the curve of the wide tractor seat. It sure felt safer up here.

Back at the farm's main area, we had some free time. The chaperones were talking in a big group near the bottom of Plumpy's hill. Ms. Merrily and the other teachers were trying to get our lunches gathered and carried over to the picnic tables.

I stood with Lauren and Sheila. "We've got to get back at those boys for what they did on the basketball court!" Sheila said, pounding a fist into her open palm.

I looked up the hill toward Plumpy. Kids, mostly boys, were running all over the slope, looking like ants on an old potato chip that had been dropped on the ground. The hill was mostly dirt and was pretty muddy because there were hoses scattered all over it. Some hoses were wound up neatly in a circle, but some were attached to faucets on the side of the barn next to the hill. These particular hoses were stretched across the slope, and some were leaking, creating little streams of muddy water that ran down the hill.

I stared at Plumpy, who was straining against the ropes that held him down.

"Hey," I said, "imagine if Plumpy came loose? He would roll right over all those boys!" I laughed as I pictured this.

Sheila looked wide-eyed up at Plumpy. Then she thumped me on the back, and I reached out to Lauren for support. "Arlene! You're a genius!"

"Yeah, I know," I grinned. "But what exactly are you talking about?"

"It's the perfect revenge. Squash those boys' smugly smiling faces right into the mud and glop! Yes, let's do it!"

"I don't get it," Lauren said.

"Let's untie Plumpy!" Sheila hissed, in that kind of shout-whisper you do when you really want to yell but can't because you don't want anyone to hear what you're saying.

"What? I didn't say we *should* untie Plumpy!" I stared at Sheila. "I said, *imagine* if he got loose. We could get in real trouble for messing with that pumpkin!"

"Nah! Who's going to see us?" Sheila said. "Come on, let's get Jessie and the other girls, and let's do this! Let's show those boys who will rule the school!"

"I don't know about this," I said. Tampering with the anchors of a giant, floating pumpkin balloon? I was certain that this would be considered unacceptable behavior for an SGA officer, or any student for that matter!

Lauren was hesitating too. "Sheila, if we get caught . . ."

But by then Jessie had been filled in on the plan. "Sheila, that's brilliant! That will definitely shut those boys up!"

"It was Arlene's idea," Sheila said.

"It wasn't, really," I stammered, "I was just saying imagine . . ."

"Arlene," Jessie said, "you thought this up? Way more boldness than I would've guessed you had. Now you're thinking like a candidate who's out to win this thing. Let's go!"

I enjoyed the short burst of pride that hit me with Jessie's sort-of compliment, but then I looked to Lauren for help out of this awful, awful situation. This was not good. This was very wrong. Lauren just returned my worried glance.

But if I didn't go along with this, Jessie would for sure think of me as a lame, loser candidate. I'd never get her and her friends' support in the election. But if I did go along with it, I might get in tremendous trouble! What would Mom say?

I shook my head violently. I had to get Mom out of my head right now, before she ruined everything. "Yeah, let's go!" I heard myself saying.

Lauren looked shocked, but she began to trudge up the side of the hill, along with the rest of the girls, out of sight of the chaperones and the unsuspecting boys.

There were decorations along the side of the slope, little things to look at while you climbed, I guessed. Like in the woods, there were cutouts of pigs and other farm animals, some pumpkins and apple bushels, and then a scarecrow with no head. This was so you could stand behind the scarecrow, put your own head on its shoulders, and take a picture.

I stayed with the girls for about a third of the way up the hill, which now seemed like a mountain to me. But then my legs ran out of energy. I told the girls I would catch up with them in a minute, to go on without me for now.

Lauren looked at me as if to say, "Are you sure?" I stared back, which told her, "Yes!"

Sheila was so focused on the top of the hill and staying out of sight of the boys that she barely noticed I had stopped climbing. But Jessie took full notice. She shook her head in disappointment topped with a hint of "I told you so."

I sighed and slung my arm across the shoulders of the headless scarecrow, leaning on my new friend to rest as I watched the girls journey toward the big, fat pumpkin. I had failed. I couldn't keep up. I was doomed in these elections. Jessie probably wouldn't vote for me now, and how long would it be before Sheila realized that I couldn't hack it? And then the rumors would just spread until my reputation was back where I started: Girl with the Leg Braces (who couldn't even make it up a stupid hill).

I did my best. It was all I could do.

And I stunk.

Just then, Byron came up to me, panting.

"Arlene, that hill is awesome! Are you going to go up? Are you tired? Did you fall or something? What's wrong?"

"Nah. I'm not going up there. Too muddy," I lied.

"Yeah, it is pretty messy."

I stared in silence toward the big pumpkin. There was a crowd of boys just under Plumpy, trying to keep their footing in the dirt and mud.

Behind Plumpy I spied Sheila, Jessie, and the other girls. Some were bent over one of the short stakes holding the ropes that kept big ole Plumpy in place. Sheila had slipped the orange tail off of the pump and was tying it tight to keep Plumpy full of air. No one, not even Byron, noticed what was going on up there.

Plumpy began to wobble. A gust of wind blew, and Plumpy swayed way too far forward. The girls ran to another stake, and Plumpy leaned even farther off his perch.

A minute later, while laughter erupted from the top of the hill, Plumpy started to freefall down. As each boy spotted the orange steamroller headed right for him, I heard more and more screaming.

Down ole Plumpy fell, and the boys dropped flat against the ground, tucked into the mud as the big balloon rolled over them. The girls danced in victory at the top of the hill. The boys popped up after Plumpy passed, shaking their muddy fists in the air.

I had to smile. Yay, girls! Even if I hadn't made it up there, and even if I had some serious doubts about this whole idea, I couldn't help but feel part of this latest act of revenge. We were even now, you silly boys!

Byron slapped his thigh with an "Oh, my gosh!" I bet he was glad that he wasn't up there. I was glad too. I didn't want to see my good friend get a mud bath. After all, Byron wasn't part of the leaf-throwing incident.

I laughed as I watched Plumpy gather speed down the hill.

But then I panicked.

Plumpy was headed right for the group of chaperones at the bottom of the hill. By the time Plumpy got down there, he would be going way too fast and have way too much force. He might really hurt someone.

And it would be all my fault! I would be responsible for a bunch of squashed chaperones!

"Byron," I shouted, "we have to stop Plumpy! Look!" I pointed downhill. He looked in horror and agreed. Those grown-ups were in trouble!

But how do you stop a humongous, rolling pumpkin? They didn't teach us this in my Girl Scouts Happy Nature Trails course!

I searched around, looking for who knows what. I had to do something. Wait! The hoses! Maybe we could make Plumpy fly up and over those grownups. We could trip him!

"Quick, Byron, lift up this hose and tie it to the scarecrow! Make, like, a big line in the air across the hill. Maybe it'll break Plumpy's fall!"

We grabbed a hose near our feet that stretched across the slope. It was attached to a faucet on the barn wall on the other side of the hill. We wrapped our end of the hose over my scarecrow friend's shoulder and chest, the way that the school safety patrols wear their bright orange belts. This created a line in the air across the slope, like a giant limbo setup. I just hoped that Plumpy would fly *over*, not under, the limbo line.

The pumpkin balloon steamed down the hill, falling faster and faster. Byron and I pulled the hose as tight as we could. I wanted to just close my eyes and exit this whole scene, but I knew I had to look. So through eyes squinted mostly shut I watched Plumpy race toward our limbo line. Then, wham! Plumpy hit the hose and bounced high into the sky, flying over the grown-ups. This enormous orange bomb soared through the air as I gripped Byron's arm, then it sailed toward the farming equipment parked behind the chaperones. I covered my wide-open mouth as I watched Plumpy crash right into Farmer Paw Sox's tractor. Plumpy burst, of course, spewing one foul-smelling breeze toward the crowd of horrified Greenwood Elementary School guests.

Well, there was certainly one big mess of confusion after the explosion, with the grownups trying to figure out what happened. Farmer Paw Sox lifted his cap and scratched his head, staring up that hill. This was a mystery that would go down in history at Plumpy Pumpkin Farms.

Ms. Merrily never found out that it was the girls who loosened the reins on ole Plumpy, or that it was— kind of—all my idea. The boys knew it was us, but they didn't want to be tattletales. They just rubbed their muddy hands together, signaling to us that they were busy plotting their next sneaky move.

But Ms. Merrily did find out, thanks to Byron, that it was me who noticed the danger for the adults, and that it was me who thought of tripping the pumpkin with the hose.

Ms. Merrily hailed me a hero, a lifesaver. Sheila agreed. She wrapped her arm around my neck and whispered in my ear, "Thanks for fixing things down here at the bottom. We would have been in big trouble without you. You rock."

Jessie, on the other hand, didn't think of me as a hero. She looked at me suspiciously as we boarded the bus. I just smiled and said nothing. She could think what she wanted. I had done my best in this crazy situation. It was all I could do.

On the ride home, Carlos slumped in his seat, staring at the seatback in front of him, looking as deflated as ole Plumpy. His hair was flattened against his skull, caked with mud. His dirt-covered cheeks bounced along with the bus as he sighed and closed his eyes. My chest felt tight. What had I gotten myself into with this election? What were the costs?

But then Carlos opened his eyes and saw me looking at him, probably with that same "Aw" look that I always get from other people. One side of Carlos' mouth spread into a wide smirk. The eyebrow on the other side of his face arched high toward his muddy hair. He shook his fist and then pointed a finger at me. "Look out," he mouthed and laughed dramatically.

Well. Guess he had no problem with the crazy game we were all playing. In fact, he looked like he was ready for round three.

Lauren was giddy as she scrunched down with me in the seat across the aisle from Carlos. "You did it, Arlene." she whispered. "I figured it was all over, but not only did we get revenge, you came out a hero. We still have a great chance in this election."

"Yeah, imagine that."

But this was no time for imagination. That was how the whole pumpkin roll got started in the first place. No, this was a time to be super alert, to be on my toes, even in my awesome purple leg braces.

IN CONTROL

The day after the pumpkin patch field trip, I felt like the most popular girl in school. Apparently, Plumpy's roll was a huge story on the Greenwood Elementary grapevine. I didn't know how people found out so fast, but even before school started, everyone had heard the story of the Attack of the Giant Pumpkin.

Generally, in the morning before school begins, students wait in the cafeteria for the first bell. We're supposed to sit on the floor in straight lines according to grade and classroom, but that's a joke. It's just one big mishmash of kids. Everyone talks and laughs about anything from homework to movies to the music teacher's latest bow tie. But today, the topic was the same for all: me. Well, me and steamrolling pumpkins.

"Arlene, good thing you were on the scene!" one kid shouted.

"Hey," yelled another, "my zucchini's outta control! Can you help me?"

Like they say, there's no such thing as bad publicity. If I made a great speech to the school next week and delivered an over-the-top presentation of my Precious Thing, I'd be in good shape for the election.

For the time being, though, I had to do my last round of PTA presentations. I wanted to go out strong, so I came up with a cheer to really get the audience involved.

In a sixth-grade classroom, I gave it my best shot:

> *"P to the Izz-oh*
> *T to the Izz-ay*
> *A to the PTA!*
> *When I say Parents, you say Teachers:*
> *Parents!"*

"*Teachers!*" the class shouted.

"Parents!"

"Teachers!" they shouted again.

"When I say PT, you say A:

"PT!"

"A!" the class yelled.

"PT!"

"A!"

"What does it spell?" I asked.

There was a moment of silent confusion.

"Puh-tah!" one guy called out.

"That's right!" I yelled. *"Puh-tah!"*

I began to clap.

"And we'll rock harder than a fat guitah.

We'll fly higher than the highest stah.

We'll roll faster than Speed Racer's cah.

Say it with me now:

P to the T to the A!

P to the T to the A!

P to the T to the A!

Lemme hear it! P!" I shouted.

The class was on their feet. *"P!"*

"And a T!" I yelled.

"T!"

"And an A!"

"A!"

I soaked in the applause. I felt like a whole new person—a performer, a star. It was a whole different side of me, and it felt like it fit. I swayed down the corridor back to my classroom, beaming bright enough to light the whole hallway.

In the classroom, Joey was up next for the Precious Things presentations. I sat back to enjoy what I was sure was going to be an interesting speech, probably one making Joey look like the king of the world.

Joey shuffled to the front of the room and turned his body toward the class, but then he looked right down at the floor. Well, that was weird. I had never seen such a slouchy king. Then Joey slipped one hand into the pocket of his baggy pants, and with the other hand, he held up a worn army jacket in front of his face.

Joey began, "This is my army jacket that—"

"Joey," Ms. Merrily called, "please hold your Precious Thing to the side, honey. We can't see you."

Joey huffed out a sigh. He moved the army jacket just slightly to his right and stuffed his hand deeper into his pants pocket.

"This is my army jacket," he began again. "My great-grandfather gave it to me. Gramps fought in World War II. He was in D-day, which was one of the biggest battles in history. No one thought the Americans could win, but they did because they were tough and smart and brave. Gramps drove a tank and got shot at. But he survived, and he told me all about it. He gave me this jacket. To keep."

Then there was silence. When Ms. Merrily figured out that Joey was finished, she remarked, "That's a great story, Joey. Does anyone have any questions?"

"Does it have any bullet holes in it?" Carlos wanted to know.

"No. I said he was in a *tank*."

"Do you have your gramps' dog tags?" Adam asked. He's a collector. He probably wanted to buy them from Joey.

"Yup. He gave those to me too. I have all his army stuff."

"So Joey, can you tell the class why this jacket is special to you?" Ms. Merrily asked.

"'Cuz it's from my gramps. He gave me this jacket to help protect me. It keeps me warm, and it's very thick, so if something came flying through the air at me, I would be safe in this jacket."

I pictured tiny objects zinging in from the ocean and onto our playground, and all of us falling to the grass in pain, all except for Joey in his oversized army jacket. I thought I should get one of those.

"You're lucky to have this gift from your great-grandfather," Ms. Merrily said. "He must be proud to see you wearing it, even if it is, well, so big for you."

"He'll never see me wear it. He's dead." Joey sucked in a breath, and then looked down quickly, shoving his hand as far as it would go into his pocket. He pressed his chin to his chest and walked quickly to his seat, slamming his body into his chair and hugging the jacket with both arms.

"Thank you, Joey, sweetie. That was a wonderful presentation. And I'm sorry to hear about your gramps. He sounds like a wonderful man. I know it must be hard for you to talk about him to the whole class."

Everyone stared at Joey. Joey answered with silence as he buried his face in his jacket. Carlos leaned over and patted his friend gently on the shoulder.

Poor Joey, I thought. Maybe he isn't such a Tough Guy after all. Maybe there's another side to him, just a regular dude who loved his gramps.

"All right, chickadees, it's time for lunch!" Ms. Merrily called. "Line up quietly as mice!"

In the cafeteria, the girls had their first chance to talk since yesterday. Lauren jumped right in. "That was wild at the pumpkin patch, wasn't it? We got those boys back! Did you see Carlos' face? He had mud all over him!"

"Yeah!" Sheila agreed. "Those boys will know not to mess with us again. And we didn't even get caught! In fact, our candidate saved the day!" Sheila slapped her palm onto my shoulder and gave it a shake.

I smiled and gripped the table. "Yeah, it worked out, didn't it?"

"But I'm just wondering," Jessie began. "Arlene, how do you get to be the hero in all this? After all, it was your big idea to do the pumpkin roll thing."

"What are you talking about?" I asked.

"I'm talking about the fact that you created that big mess, then you turned everything around and saved the day. It's like you set *us* up to take all the risk, then you made yourself the hero."

"I didn't make myself anything!" I protested. "I had no idea that the stupid pumpkin was going to crush the chaperones. I had to do something! Did you expect me to just stand there and watch?"

"Yeah, Jessie," said Lauren. "It's a good thing that Arlene did what she did. She saved lives!"

"Look," Jessie said, "all I'm saying is, why wasn't Arlene at the top of the hill with the rest of us?"

"Yeah, that's true," Sheila said. "I thought you were coming up there with us."

I pressed my lips together. I didn't want to say it. It might ruin everything. If I admitted I was the soldier who fell behind, where would that leave me?

But there was nothing else to say, except the truth.

"I couldn't make it up the hill. OK? You happy now?" I glared at Jessie.

Jessie lowered her eyes and shrugged casually. "That's what I figured," she said. Then she looked up and met my glare head-on.

There was silence for a moment. Sheila examined her pretzel sticks. Lauren looked frantic, probably trying to think of something to smooth this all over. I crossed my arms and prepared to stay in this staring contest for the rest of lunch. Lucky for my unblinking, dry eyes, the recess bell rang after just a minute or so. We all got up from the table, and I walked one way, Jessie another.

I would have to be careful with Jessie, because I couldn't afford to have a huge fight with her in the middle of the election and lose a whole bunch of votes. I had to try to keep the peace, just like Lauren would, as much as I hated doing it.

That night, as I tried to get to sleep, I lay in my bed looking at that Monet painting Mom made a big deal about the other day. I looked at the thousands of tiny, colored strokes that made up the big picture. What strokes, I wondered, made up the big picture of me?

Sometimes it feels like CMT has splashed a big purple stripe right across my life—just one big, blinding streak. But this year, one stroke at a time, I was coloring over it, making it a smaller and smaller part of me. And this made me feel like I could control the universe.

I became an SGA candidate—swish! I was a hit as PTA spokesperson—splotch! I saved the day at the pumpkin patch—splatch! If that Jessie would stop pointing out the leftover traces of my disability every chance she gets, I thought, I'll be all set. I can win this election and finally prove something.

That I'm just like everyone else.

GLAMOUR GIRL

The next morning, after the bell rang for us to go to our classrooms, that PTA lady, Mrs. Landers, came up to me.

"Arlene, I just wanted to thank you for doing such a great job as PTA Membership Drive Spokesperson. Our membership is up 35 percent from last year. We've never had a more successful spokesperson! You brought creativity and pizzazz to the job. Thank you!"

I wasn't sure what *pizzazz* was. Maybe it was part of some secret PTA code language. Anyway, this lady was pleased with me, and that was good.

I used my best talking-to-a-grown-up voice, like Mom taught me. "Thank you, Mrs. Landers. I'm happy to help. I had a lot of fun."

Mrs. Landers leaned down and pinched my cheek. "You are welcome, honey. I'll look for you next year!"

"You bet!" I smiled and went on my way to my classroom. I remembered the look on Mrs. Landers' face back when I was first picked as PTA Spokesperson. But she no longer looked at me with that "Aw" expression. My plan was working.

Back in Room 22, I could feel the tension between the boys and the girls. It was like one of those fogs that drifts into town from the beaches in the early morning. I noticed Joey and Sheila shooting mean looks at each other. I saw Maddie throw a paper at Carlos instead of handing it to him. And I caught Lauren tossing Spencer's library book aside before she brought the class bucket of book returns to the library.

It felt like a time bomb was ticking in our class. The question was when, not if, the whole thing would explode in our faces.

Ms. Merrily didn't seem to notice anything. She paid attention to the simple things, to the merry stuff. But this was politics. This was war. And it wasn't pretty, or merry.

After math and reading, it was Jessie's turn for the Precious Things presentations. I figured she would bring in her favorite dress or purse or something.

Jessie walked proudly to the front of the room. She pulled her hair off her face and wrapped it in an orange scrunchie that matched the pattern of tiny flowers on her sun-yellow shirt. Her pants were the color of beach sand. She looked like she had just stepped off the pages of a travel brochure for the Caribbean islands. No matter what had happened between us, I had to admit, she looked awesome.

Jessie reached behind her with both hands and unhooked her necklace. She held it up high and turned this way and that to show everyone in the class. It was a silver chain with a heart charm. Well, half a heart. The heart was split in a zig-zagged way down the middle, and it had the word "Friends" engraved on it. The other half of the heart was missing.

"This is my most precious possession, this beautiful necklace," Jessie began.

Now this was what I would have expected, jewelry. What else from a Glamour Girl?

"My best friend has the other half of the heart, which says *Best*. And if you put the halves together, they spell out *Best Friends*."

I waited for Jessie to name Maddie or some other Glamour Girl as the owner of the other half.

"Bernadine, who is my best friend, has the other half. Well, I get to call her Bernie because I know her so well. She lives in Massachusetts, where she goes to college. She is twenty-one years old. She used to be my babysitter, but now she's my best friend in the whole world. In fact, she's my role model."

Well, this was unexpected. And interesting too.

Jessie went on, "Bernie plays soccer for Boston College. She's really, really good at it. Whenever she comes home, she always visits me. And the last time she came home she gave me this necklace because she says she thinks about me even when she's away at college. I want to be an athlete just like her when I grow up because she's so cool. And that's why this is my most Precious Thing."

I rubbed my eyes and squinted toward the front of the room. Great story, but who was that up there? It couldn't be Jessie, number-one Glamour Girl. Did she just say that she wanted to *play sports* when she got older?

"That's a lovely necklace, Jessie," Ms. Merrily said. "That must make you feel so good inside, having a wonderful best friend like Bernadine. Does anyone have any questions for Jessie?"

Of course we did. The boys asked what position Bernie played, how many goals she scored this year, and all sorts of sports stuff.

Didn't anyone see how weird this was, coming from Jessie? Wasn't anyone going to challenge her? She certainly would have questioned me on something like this. But then again, she did seem to have something against me in particular. Ms. Merrily eventually cut off the questioning and told us to get ready for lunch and recess.

I walked slowly toward the cubby room, thinking about Jessie's presentation. Everyone was surprising me with their Precious Things. It felt like I didn't really know anybody at all.

I stopped just outside the cubbies to say hello to Ketchup and Mustard. They were sleeping soundly in their log. As I watched the class pets, I wondered if I should say something to Jessie. She just gave a great presentation, and questioning her would just stir things up. Maybe I should just leave things peaceful, like our little gerbil friends here.

I went into the cubby room and saw Spencer and Byron gathering their jackets to take to the cafeteria. I said, "Hey, guys!" but only Byron answered me. Spencer eyed me with suspicion.

Then Jessie and Maddie came in. Spencer slammed his back against the wall and spread his arms wide, like he needed to create as much space as possible between himself and the creatures that just walked in. He slinked along the wall until he got to the door, and then he bolted. Byron imitated his friend, crying "Ahhh!" and running back out into the classroom.

Jessie rolled her eyes. "They're still mad, I guess," she said and gently elbowed Maddie.

Maddie nodded. "Well, when you're losers, what else are you going to do but run away?"

Jessie raised her hand to Maddie for a high five. "Got that right, girl."

Hey, I was in on this too. I raised my hand for a high five. "You know it," I said.

Jessie sighed and touched my hand with hers the way I touch the cloth to my face when ordered to wash up: barely.

"What's our next move?" I asked, still trying to be part of this little war council.

"I don't know for sure, but I know it's going to be big," Maddie replied.

"Bigger than an exploding pumpkin?" I said.

"Maybe," Jessie said. "It might be something that you won't be able to do, Arlene. I mean, you can't be in on everything. War is rough. You couldn't even get up the hill at the pumpkin patch." And she looked right at my awesome purple leg braces.

OK, I had enough. Any doubt about challenging this girl just flew right out the window. Brace yourselves, Ketchup and Mustard, things are about to be stirred up!

I crossed my arms. "What do you mean, I can't do everything? I can do anything I want to!"

Jessie, her eyes half closed, just shrugged.

"Oh, yeah," I challenged. "What makes you think you can be an athlete, huh, Jessie? I mean, you might get your clothes all dirty and your hair all messed up." I waved my finger in the air around Jessie's head. "Won't that ruin your whole look, Glamour Girl?"

Jessie's eyes popped open wide, and she glared at me. "If you're trying to say that all I care about is how I look, then you obviously didn't listen to what I just told everyone. How dare you stand there and judge me, calling me names. You, of all people!"

My cheeks heated up, and my stomach flipped. I actually felt my fingers start to curl into a fist. Was I going to try to give this girl a right hook? I took a deep breath but couldn't think of anything to say. It was like my anger was fogging up my brain.

Lauren came into the cubby room and looked at me, then at Jessie, then back at me again. "What's going on?" she said carefully.

"Nothing!" Jessie snapped, and she stuffed her hair into her scrunchie, grabbed her jacket, and stomped back into the classroom.

"Whoa, what happened in here?" Lauren asked.

I rubbed my face to try to clear my head. "Jessie's just crazy," I mumbled. I took my jacket and left the cubby room. I didn't want to talk about this, even to Lauren, until I could really think it through.

Was I judging Jessie? I was sure it was the other way around, that she was judging me! I mean, after all, wasn't she the one who said I couldn't win the SGA election? Wasn't she the one who kept saying that I couldn't handle all this war stuff? That sounded like a big, fat judger to me.

But I had never said *Glamour Girl* out loud before. That probably did hurt her feelings. I didn't mean to do that, but she made me mad so many times in the last few weeks! I just couldn't hold it in any longer.

Now I was worried, too, about how this would affect the election. What if Jessie was dead-set against me now? What if she tried to ruin my campaign?

A SECRET PLAN

I was still feeling pretty unsettled on the day of my Precious Things presentation. I hadn't spoken to Jessie since our showdown in the cubby room the day before, so I couldn't tell if things had changed, if she was supporting me in the election or not. With our class divided in half because of this war, even one or two votes could be very important. There was a lot riding on my presentation.

At lunch, I was glad to hustle to the cafeteria and sit down with Lauren. I felt safe and comfortable with her. I took out the sandwich that Dad had made for me that morning. It was just the way I liked it: two pieces of ham, lots and lots of mustard, and that yellow egg bread. It took some time to train Dad to make me the perfect lunch, but he's an eager learner. He has potential. Now if I can just convince him to substitute cookies for these carrot sticks, we'll be all set.

Lauren was picking at her string cheese. "Where's Byron?" I asked.

"Oh, I think he's buying lunch."

"Really?" I said. "I thought he hated all cafeteria food except pizza."

I looked up and down the long table where our class sat. Almost all of the boys were missing. Sure, they were serving tacos, a pretty popular meal on the Greenwood menu, but still, Byron bought lunch only when they served pizza.

"Well, where are all the other guys?" I asked.

Lauren looked up and down the rows. "Huh, that's weird. Guess they're all buying lunch today."

We continued to munch on our food and talk about the looming SGA elections. We were going to hear speeches from all of the candidates on Monday at the assembly, and then vote in the afternoon. First thing on Tuesday we would find out who won.

"Can you believe it, Arlene?" Lauren said. "By next week, you could be an SGA officer!"

"Yeah," I said, trying to calculate how many votes I would be short if I lost the Glamour Girls.

"I think you have a real shot. Everyone has heard about what you did at the pumpkin patch. You're like, famous. And besides that, everyone loved your rhymes and songs during the PTA Membership Drive. You've become more popular than Mr. Peterson, the janitor!"

And that was a hard thing to do, to be more popular than Mr. Peterson. He was the friendliest guy on the planet. He must have been eighty years old, but he was still pushing his wide broom through the halls of Greenwood, smiling and high-fiving kids left and right.

"Speaking of popular," I said. "I'm worried about Jessie. Have you talked to her?"

"No. But you never told me what happened between you two in the cubby room yesterday. What's up?"

"Well, she might be all mad at me because I called her a *Glamour Girl*."

"You what?" Lauren tried her best to look upset, but then she burst out laughing. I joined her and, whew, did I feel better!

"Arlene!" Lauren said as she tried to keep a straight face. "Arlene, that wasn't the best campaign strategy!"

"I know, but you saw how she kept attacking me, with all those shrugs and comments and eye rolls!" I demonstrated each of these for Lauren, and she started cracking up again.

"It's true," Lauren said. "It does seem like she has some kind of problem with you. But jeez, couldn't you have waited 'til after Monday to start calling people names?"

I sighed. "Too late now."

We were finishing up our lunches, and the boys still hadn't shown up. I turned around to look at the tables behind me.

There they were, a group of boys from our class, at a table way in the back of the cafeteria, far from any of the lunch aides or teachers. They were all squashed together at one end of the table. Something was definitely going on. Joey was directing things, of course, and Byron seemed to be the lookout. They all looked very serious, like this was an important, top-secret mission.

"The boys are up to something," I said. "Look."

While Lauren turned around to check them out, I tapped on the shoulder of Sheila, who was sitting down the bench from me. Soon, a bunch of us girls were spying on those boys at the back of the cafeteria.

"Yeah, they're definitely up to something," Sheila said. "That is just too weird, all of them back there, crowding around a bunch of tacos."

Jessie slid down the bench to join our conversation. I felt my neck muscles tighten, but I didn't say anything to her. I figured I would play it cool, let her make the first move.

She ignored me. "We need a spy!" she said and threw her napkin at Maddie. "Throw this away, girl!"

Maddie giggled and walked slowly to the trash can near the end of the boys' table. Byron saw her and shouted, "Munch-a-lunch!" (It must have been some sort of code.) All of the boys sat up straight. Carlos and Byron moved to form a wall between the end of the table and the trash can.

Wow, these boys were organized. Maddie couldn't see a thing.

She walked back to our table. "I couldn't see a thing," she said and tossed the napkin back at Jessie.

"Now what am I supposed to do with this, Maddie?" Jessie said. "At least throw the thing away!"

"Oops, sorry!" Maddie giggled.

I was kind of worried. "Do you think they're going to do something to mess up my presentation after recess?" I wondered aloud.

"Don't worry," Sheila said. "You've got all of us behind you, Arlene."

I watched Jessie carefully. All of the girls behind me, huh? I wondered whether that was true.

The girls of Room 22 squashed themselves into a big group at the end of the table.

"We've got to find out what those boys are up to, and we need to stop them!" Sheila said as she pounded her big fist on the table.

"We can't let anything happen to Arlene," Lauren added.

I felt so good and confident just yesterday morning, when I talked with Mrs. Landers. But now something horrible and embarrassing might happen to me while

I did my Precious Things presentation. Everything could be totally ruined!

Oh, man! Mom might be right! This war thing is wrong, stupid, no good. Someone might get hurt. And that someone might be me!

But how do you stop a war without surrendering, without losing?

THE BEST DEFENSE

At recess, we tried to uncover whatever evil plan the boys had cooked up. We all had our assignments. I watched for any signs of suspicious activity on the playground. Sheila and Lauren played basketball, but really, they watched over the courts and black-top. Jessie and Maddie covered the field.

I spotted Byron by the door to the gym. I figured I would check out what he was doing. He was my best way into the enemy camp. I walked toward him, but before I reached him, Spencer burst through the door. He ran over to Byron, and Joey and Carlos joined them.

Whoa, something was up. I ducked behind a tree, doing my best spy imitation.

Spencer paused in front of the boys, for dramatic effect or something. His eyes were dead serious, his hands were planted on his hips, and he had his legs spread apart. If he were wearing a cape, he would have looked like a superhero.

"It is done," he pronounced in his deepest voice.

There was a pause as this news sank in. Then the boys cheered: "Yeah! All right! Way to go, Spence!" They slapped Spencer on his back, hugged him, and just generally shoved each other around.

Yeah, I'll never understand boy language.

But this didn't sound good. I wondered what "it" was, and what did it mean that it was "done?" Was "it" raw before, and now it was cooked? Was Spencer grilling hamburgers inside the school?

No, I was sure this was part of their evil plan. I ran over to Sheila and Lauren. "Hey, guys! Something weird just happened."

The girls stopped their basketball game and gathered around me. "What's up, Arlene?" Sheila said. "Spill it."

"Spencer just came out of the school and said to all the boys, *It is done*," I told them.

"It is done," murmured Lauren. We girls stood together, trying to decode this strange message. Jessie must have seen us gathered on the court, because she came over too.

Sheila said, "Hey, Jessie. I'm going to say three words to you, and I want you to tell me the first thing that comes to your mind. OK? Ready?"

Jessie nodded.

Sheila took a deep breath and said, "It is done."

Sheila stepped back to give Jessie room to respond. The rest of us leaned forward a little and waited for Jessie's answer, like she was some kind of genius who was about to announce the meaning of life itself.

Jessie looked a little blank. Then she shrugged and said, "Great. When do we eat?"

"Oh!" we all groaned. This was no help at all. She must have thought the same thing I did, that there was some sort of roasting going on in the school.

"It has to have something to do with my presentation," I said. "That makes the most sense. If they've set something up in the classroom, some sort of trap or something, it probably has to do with me."

"You're right," Sheila said. "Girls, we've got to figure this out. What could they do to Arlene during her presentation?"

I thought about my good friend Byron, and even Joey and Carlos, who I really liked. And I thought about me, standing up there alone in front of the class, in my purple leg braces with floating butterflies. "Would they really do something to *me?*" I said.

"What? Because you've got those leg braces on?" Jessie was back, looking more fierce than ever. "Now, all of a sudden, everyone is supposed to notice you've got leg braces on? Which way do you want it, Arlene?" Jessie flung her hair back into a fluorescent yellow scrunchie. "Look, this is what I've been saying all along. You're in way over your head."

"I am not!" I said. "For your information, Jessie, I'm not talking about my leg braces. I don't want something crazy and embarrassing to happen while I'm up there doing my presentation. It'll ruin my chances in the election!"

Lauren jumped to my defense. "Yeah, Jessie. This is about those crazy scheming boys. We can't back down now! But we can't let anything happen to Arlene either. Would they really stoop that low and mess up Arlene's presentation?"

"Oh, they'll stoop." Sheila said. "We can't take any chances." She puffed her chest out and sliced her hands through the air in front of her in karate chop fashion. "There is no way anyone is going to mess with any one of us. Just let those boys try it! They won't know what hit 'em when we get through!"

"Maybe we could disrupt the class enough so that Arlene doesn't get called up to do her presentation," suggested Maddie. "That way we can watch and see what they do, what they say. I'll bet that if Arlene doesn't get called up, one of those boys will reveal what their plan was."

"You're absolutely right!" Sheila exclaimed. "That's a perfect plan, a perfect setup. Yes, we have to do something totally disruptive."

Everyone put their thinking caps on, as Ms. Merrily would say.

I raised my hand slightly, like I was in class. "I don't think I'm up for doing something totally disruptive."

Sheila looked at me with that "Aw" look. Darn it! I don't want *her* to feel sorry for me!

I added quickly, "'Cuz I'm the one who's going to be called up to the front of the room. I'm the target of the attack! I can't also create the distraction!"

There. Good excuse for not doing something totally disruptive, without making them feel all sorry for me.

Sheila nodded. "You're right, Arlene. You can't be a part of this. Don't worry. Disruption is my specialty."

SLIPPING AND SLIDING

Back inside the classroom, the air was thick, filled with suspicion. Sheila hadn't told me what she had planned, in order to protect me from any trouble, and all these unknowns were making me pretty nervous. We put our jackets away and were fooling around like always, waiting for the direction that we knew was coming: "Be quiet!" But we probably wouldn't listen until Ms. Merrily had said it at least three times.

As I walked out of the cubby room, I glanced to my right, toward the home of Ketchup and Mustard. I wanted to steer clear of whatever disruptive things were about to be set up in the classroom. I figured I would just tap on the glass of my furry little friends—wait a minute! Where were the gerbils?

They were not in their log, not buried in their wood chips, not eating or drinking or attempting to climb the glass walls of their cage. They were nowhere to be found.

Was this what had been "done?" Were the gerbils running around the classroom somewhere? But how would that get back at us girls, and what did the gerbils have to do with what had been going on in the cafeteria?

As I tried to figure all this out, the third call to "Be quiet!" came, and this time Ms. Merrily meant business. I knew this because she walked toward our chart of green, yellow, and red cards, as if she were about to start flipping some over. Kids scrambled to their seats, bumping into each other and into desks and chairs. Finally we were all settled, although some of the boys were giggling behind hands clamped over their mouths.

Ms. Merrily called out, "Arlene, are you ready to give your presentation now?"

Several boys lost the battle to hold in their laughter, and bursts of spit flew through the cracks between their fingers, followed by intense coughing to cover up the giggles. I rose slowly out of my seat, looking around, waiting for the boys' trap—whatever it was—to spring into action. Would a hole open up in the floor? Would a bucket of green slime rain down on my head? What already? Just get it over with!

And where was *my* crew? I thought Sheila and the other girls had some totally disruptive plan. When would that happen?

"Hey!" Sheila shouted. "Where are Ketchup and Mustard?"

Ms. Merrily looked confused. She stood up and walked toward the gerbil cage. After peering inside for a moment, she turned around slowly.

"Hmm, where *are* you, Ketchup and Mustard?" she sang, as if this were an ordinary question, like these rodents disappeared all the time and returned when someone called their names. "Where are you?"

No one said a word. The boys looked at each other and communicated through a complicated series of eye rolls, shoulder shrugs, and hand motions. With his forehead wrinkled, like he was part confused and part angry, Joey looked at Spencer. Spencer shrugged and looked at Carlos. Carlos pointed his finger toward Spencer, as if to say, "It's all your fault."

Sheila smiled proudly. Clearly, she was responsible for the gerbils' disappearance. So this was the disruption, runaway rodents. But the question still remained: What had the boys done?

I stood near my desk, waiting to see what was going to happen next.

Ms. Merrily walked quickly over to the intercom and pressed the button hard. "Mr. Musgrove? This is Ms. Merrily. We have a problem here in Room 22. It seems our gerbils have escaped from their cage."

"What?" Mr. Musgrove's voice blasted through the speaker. "Ms. Merrily, this is not acceptable. We have children in other classrooms who are allergic to these animals. You need to get those things back in that cage immediately."

Ms. Merrily's eyes grew big, and her face reddened. She snatched the phone that's attached to the intercom and spoke softly and urgently, but I couldn't hear what she was saying.

After a moment, she put down the phone and turned to face the class.

Wow! I could never have imagined this kind of look on Ms. Merrily's face. Her eyes were little narrow slits, and her head was straight up and down, not tilted to the side like usual. In fact, if anything, she was tilted a bit toward us, in a kind of scary way. Was she *angry*?

Yep. She spoke through clenched teeth. "These gerbils need to be returned to their cage, *right now*. If any student in this class is responsible for them being out of their cage, I will deal with you later, but believe me, I will deal with you. Right now, the *only* thing anybody should be doing is *finding those gerbils*!"

We all snapped into action. Everyone began running around the classroom again, looking under tables, behind bookshelves, anywhere a gerbil could hide. Some kids were calling, "Here Ketchup! Here Mustard!" and some held out sunflower seeds. We had to find those rodents fast!

Ms. Merrily scrambled more than anyone else. She must have been in big trouble with Mr. Musgrove. When we heard the clopping of Mr. Musgrove's fancy shoes coming down the hall, Ms. Merrily's head popped up from under her desk, where she was looking for the gerbils.

"Is he coming here?" she asked no one in particular.

The door burst open, and Mr. Musgrove entered the room. "OK," he said as he strode across the front of the classroom toward Ms. Merrily, who was just beginning to stand up from crouching under her desk. "We have a big problem here—"

Before he could finish his sentence Mr. Musgrove slipped, and *whoosh,* across the floor he went. He must ski up in the mountains of Vermont or something, because that guy had great balance. He kind of turned sideways, like he was surfing, and held his balance almost all the way across the front of the room.

Almost.

Just before he collided into Ms. Merrily and her desk, I thought, *That's* what the boys were up to! Taco grease! Ewww!

Then, crash! Mr. Musgrove banged into Ms. Merrily, and they both stumbled and crumbled to the floor near her desk. They lay there on the floor in a heap for a moment, and I looked at Mr.

Musgrove's face, all squished with embarrassment and probably a little pain.

That could have been me. That should have been me. I felt downright sick.

I had wanted to be a part of a war. I had wanted to be just like the other kids. And I forgot about everything else, everything I knew about what was right and what was wrong. Boy, did I mess up, big time.

As Mr. Musgrove gathered his long legs into a position where he could hoist himself off of Ms. Merrily, Ketchup revealed himself. Or at least I thought it was Ketchup. He and Mustard were hard to tell apart.

Ketchup made a grand appearance, right on top of Ms. Merrily's blond head. As if to say, "Ta-da!" he stood on his hind legs and looked out at the class. I could have sworn he was smiling.

Mustard, or whichever one he was, was not far behind. He ran up the loose sleeve of Mr. Musgrove's suit jacket, which made Mr. Musgrove leap to his feet and jump up and down to try to get the animal out of his clothing.

At this point, we all woke up from our shock and started chasing our class pets. Kids were running all over the room trying to catch them. Ms. Merrily was taking a moment to recover. Mr. Musgrove had gotten the gerbil out of his sleeve, but he didn't catch him.

So with two gerbils on the loose and a small storm of activity brewing in the classroom, Mr. Musgrove held up his two hands high in the air and shouted, "That is it! Everyone to your seats! Now!"

We all followed orders. This guy clearly meant business. He took control, as any good principal would have done in this situation. He ushered Ms. Merrily to the nurse to be checked over and to "take a breather." He split our class into two groups and sent each one to a different classroom. He told us that our classroom would be put back in order by Mr. Peterson and himself, and then "we would get to the bottom of this."

I wondered what would be "at the bottom." Probably a whole heap of trouble for all of us. I imagined indoor recess and writing assignments for the rest of our lives. Or scrubbing the bathrooms with a toothbrush like I'd seen in some army movie that Chris watched. Maybe four-mile jogs around the playground with our backpacks on, singing, "I don't know but I've been told, we'll run out here 'til we grow old."

It turned out, the bottom included a whole bunch of red cards, one for each student in the class. Then, during a long classroom meeting, the whole story came out, how this boy-girl war had started as part of the SGA election campaign and then spread like the flu throughout our classroom, how the disaster at the pumpkin patch had been part of it, and how the final act of revenge by the boys—collecting taco grease into a plastic container and pouring it on the floor of the classroom—had backfired and hit Mr. Musgrove and Ms. Merrily instead of me.

I was right about the indoor recess too. We were going to spend the next three weeks staying indoors and writing quiet essays about appropriate behavior, respect, and making good choices. And letters went home to all of our parents, that very day.

Obviously, I was worried about how this would affect the SGA elections. But in a separate meeting that Carlos and I had with Mr. Musgrove, it looked like everything would be OK. From what Mr. Musgrove knew, I was the victim here, at least in this latest boy-girl battle. Ms. Merrily confirmed that I was indeed the taco grease target.

And there was that "Aw" look again from Mr. Musgrove, as if he were thinking: How could the target be some poor girl in leg braces? He was focusing on this last battle and didn't seem to want to know about all I had done along the way. I really didn't want to play the sympathy card *again,* but what else could I do in this situation?

I looked over at Carlos sitting next to me in Mr. Musgrove's office. What was he going to do? Carlos was looking at Mr. Musgrove very seriously, nodding his head at all of the right moments. But when Mr. Musgrove picked up his phone for a moment, Carlos glanced at me and winked.

He was no help! I was feeling very confused about my actions during this whole election campaign. But it didn't seem to make sense for me to give some huge confession at this point. We were all in trouble. Why should I go out of my way to convince Mr. Musgrove that I deserved more punishment than everyone else? That seemed pointless.

In the end, Carlos and I silently agreed to the same strategy: shut up and let Mr. Musgrove do what he was going to do.

And what he did was tell us in his most stern principal voice that if something like this boy-girl war ever started brewing again, it would absolutely be our responsibility to tell an adult in charge immediately.

Carlos and I nodded solemnly and vowed to do so.

And because nothing specifically could be pinned on me or Carlos, we were allowed to continue participating in the SGA elections. Whew!

I just wondered what to do about this big glob of guilt that was still sitting in the pit of my stomach.

I would have to talk to the girls about working out some sort of peace treaty or something. I was absolutely done with this boy-girl war.

A TRUCE?

"OK, so how do we end this war thing?" I asked the girls. All I got in response was a bunch of shrugs.

We were all sitting in the cafeteria on Friday, eating our lunches. Lunch was the only free time we would have for the next few weeks, since recess had been replaced with all that essay writing. My Precious Things presentation was postponed until after the SGA elections. Ms. Merrily said that I needed a break, with all that had happened and with my SGA speech coming up. I figured she was the one who needed a break. She had given us busy work all morning, and for the afternoon we were going to watch a video on preserving ocean wildlife. Teachers really had a great job.

Well, except when the class gerbils get loose in the middle of a student war, and you get tackled by your principal. I guess that wasn't so much fun for her.

"Maybe we can call for a truce," I suggested to the girls.

"What does the *truth* have to do with anything here?" Sheila wanted to know.

Lauren laughed. "Not the *truth*. A *truce*," she pointed out. "It's when each side gets something they want, and each side gives up something. You know, it all works out."

"But I don't want to give up anything," Sheila said.

"I really think it's time for this war to end," I said. Then I hesitated, just for a second, because I didn't want to seem wimpy. But I pictured poor Ms. Merrily's face, and I was sure that I was right. I went ahead and said what was on my mind. "We can't do any more of this revenge stuff. I mean, trying to win this election is one thing, but the craziness that happened yesterday, well, that's a whole other thing. People could have really gotten hurt."

There was silence. Everyone was thinking about what I said. I suspected also that each girl was waiting to see how the others would respond.

Lauren was first to back me up. "Arlene is right. Enough already. It got us all into trouble. It'll just keep getting worse and worse, and soon we'll never be able to do anything. Let's just concentrate on the election campaign—the right way."

Then Maddie chimed in, "Yeah, let's forget it."

Sheila sighed. "Fine." Then she quickly added, "But we won."

I thought I had persuaded the group to go my way, but one person dashed my hopes. Guess who it was.

"Why is it over because you say it's over?" Jessie said, adding her crankiness to the conversation. "You didn't win the election yet, Arlene. No one said you're in charge."

I was not going to back down. I was right, and I knew it. "OK, so should we all be listening to you instead?" I asked Jessie. "If you wanted to be in charge of this whole election campaign, you should've run for SGA yourself. What're you, jealous or something?"

"First of all, I'm not jealous of *you*." She spat out the word "you" the same way I spit out the crunchy black seeds that are not supposed to be in my seedless watermelon. "And second of all, I think we should end this war thing too. I just don't like taking directions from people like you who couldn't handle getting to the top of that hill and who just make everyone feel sorry for them whenever it's useful and who made us take all the risks while keeping their little nosy-nose clean the whole time."

OK, I couldn't follow that run-on sentence if I tried, but I did hear the words "couldn't handle," "everyone feels sorry for," and "nosy-nose," whatever that meant. I had *had* it with Jessie!

"Can you, for once, think of something different to say? Arlene can't do this. She can't do that. Blah, blah, blah!" I shouted. "Why don't you take your big mouthy mouth, and that tiny brainy brain of yours, and just get lost!"

No one said a word. It felt like the entire cafeteria was silent.

The quiet was crushing me, so I somehow found the strength to keep talking. But my voice was starting to get shaky. "We were all in this together from the start. We were supposed to be on the same team. I'm just like everyone else here!"

"No," Jessie said quietly. "You're not. You want to quit this war thing because you can't handle it." She stopped, for just a second. And then she delivered her final, knockout blow. "You really should just quit the whole election."

My eyes filled with tears. Quickly, before they spilled over, I stood and left the table. I couldn't let anyone see how upset I was, especially Jessie. I wanted nothing to do with anybody at school.

At that moment, I really regretted getting involved in this whole scene.

LIVING IT

It was Saturday, and I got up at seven. The busy week's events left me with spinning thoughts and jumpy feelings. I wandered around the house, looking for something crunchy to eat, so my mouth would match my mood. Plus, my crunching might wake up someone else. The cereal boxes were on a shelf out of my reach, and no way could I stand on a chair. Luckily, Chris had left a bag of pretzels open on the kitchen table. Good ol' Chris. You could always count on his forgetfulness. I crunched away and waited for someone to get up.

I felt like going somewhere today, to keep my brain from thinking about all that had happened.

Finally, I heard noises from my parents' room. Without my braces on yet, I wobbled down the hall, almost falling because I tried to step *over* Chris' football pads instead of going around them. Bad ole Chris!

I thankfully reached Mom and Dad's room safely and poked my head in. I tried to move like a spy because I wasn't sure what kind of mood my parents would be in. They weren't very happy to find out from the principal's letter that the boy-girl war had still been going on. But I had explained that it was all over, that I had learned my lesson, and that Mom had been right about this whole war thing from the start. I did lose TV privileges for a week because of my role in the war, but I actually didn't mind. In a weird way, having some kind of punishment made my guilt glob feel a little smaller.

Dad was folding laundry on the big bed. I sent up a test balloon: "Good morning!" I chirped.

Dad smiled, "Hey there!"

OK, safe to move on to the next level. I found Mom in the bathroom, sitting in front of the mirror with her makeup spread out before her. She held the mascara wand with her mouth and dipped it into the bottle, which she held with both of her hands. With the wand between her lips, she lifted her head, and then she raised one hand and stuck the wand between her index and middle fingers. Finally, not being able to make her hand move at the wrist by itself, she jerked her arm so that her hand flipped from palm down to palm up. As she leaned her elbow on the counter, the mascara wand was in the perfect position between her fingers. Using both arms as a guide and with little movements of her head, she applied the color to her lashes perfectly.

I love to watch Mom get ready for the day. People have no idea how many extra steps she has to take to get to the same place they are. But that's my mom.

Sometimes, like this morning, it seems like it takes forever for her to get ready. "Mom, you almost done?"

"Yes. Why? You have an important date?" She grinned and waved the mascara brush at me.

"Ahh, get that away!"

"Well, don't mess with me then." She leaned over to give me a big kiss on my cheek. "And good morning to you."

Wow, a good night's sleep seemed to improve everyone's mood!

"Mom," I said, "do you ever feel like you can't do everything that everyone else does? I mean, you seem to always figure out a way to get things done, like this makeup stuff. But are there ever times when you just say, forget it, I can't do it?"

"Sure, Arlene. But that happens to everybody. You think your father can keep track of everyone's schedule? No way. That's my job. Or do you think Chris can make up poems and rhymes like you can? Not a chance. And yes, there are some things I'm just not going to do. Not going to do ballet, or finish a triathlon, or even go grocery shopping by myself. But that's just the way life goes."

"But if there are regular things that you can't do," I said, "like go grocery shopping, then sometimes that makes people feel sorry for you. Then boom, you become all *different*. Then you're an outsider, and before you know it, you're a freak."

Mom put the mascara bottle down and turned her chair slowly to face me. "What is going on in that big brain of yours, Arlene?"

I sighed forcefully. "It's just this girl Jessie at school. She keeps telling me I can't do things, that I'm different, that I'm not like everyone else."

"Well, that's true."

"What?" Those words hurt my ears. "But I can do anything anyone else can do!"

"No, Arlene, you can't. You can do things that you set your mind to, things that you want to do, but you cannot do anything and everything. No one can. Your disability is a part of you. It doesn't make you a *freak*. But it does affect what you can and can't do."

"Well, I wish it wouldn't. I wish I weren't so different. I wish I didn't have CMT." I held my breath as those words floated into the air between me and my mother. I never said this out loud before, and I wasn't sure what would happen next.

After a long pause Mom said, "I know, honey. Believe me, I know. But you and I do have CMT, and we can't erase that. We've got to figure out how to live it."

"You mean how to live *with* it."

"No, how to live it. How to do what we want to do, leg braces, wheelchairs, and all. How to set our goals high and reach them as best we can, in our own way. That's what I mean by *living it*."

Mom moved closer to me. "But that doesn't mean that you do everything your friends do. You need to know your limitations—just don't let other people limit you."

"But sometimes I can't figure out where my limits are," I said. "What am I supposed to do then?"

Mom went nose to nose with me, like we were two seals. "That's why you have parents, silly. Once in a while, I do know what I'm talking about."

A giggle bubbled up and popped out of my mouth, although my shoulders still felt heavy. A lot of stuff was still spinning around in my head.

"OK, my girl," Mom said. "What do you want to do today? After reading that letter from Mr. Musgrove yesterday, I'm thinking you need a good old-fashioned family day, to get you back on track."

My thoughts exactly. I'd had enough of hurtful people like Jessie. I needed some family time to set me straight again.

"I want to go to the zoo," I said. "Can we? It's a nice day, and it's only going to get colder. We haven't been since my class field trip last spring. And since the pumpkin patch disaster, Greenwood is probably banned from all field-trip sites in Rhode Island for a long time."

"Hmm," Mom said. She was definitely giving it serious thought. "Hold on. Let me talk to Dad."

Before too long we were in our van, zooming up Route 95 and into Providence: the Big City. Well, at least for Rhode Island it was the Big City.

We had a great time at the Roger Williams Park Zoo. It felt awesome to take a break from school, from the pressure of the upcoming elections, and most of all, from Jessie. It was great to just hang out with my family.

I didn't want this day to end. "Let's go explore the park!" I suggested.

Mom was really into it too. I could tell. We were dancing to the same beat today.

"Yes, that's a great idea, Arlene," she said. "Come on, hon. Let's drive around the park and see the sites."

Dad didn't look as thrilled as us girls, but he agreed. He knew better than to argue with Mom, especially when it came to family time. Mom was pretty firm about the importance of this.

We rode by the sights of the park: the Casino, a fancy mansion where people could have parties and weddings; the Temple to Music, where they held outdoor concerts in the summer; and the statue of Roger Williams, the guy who helped start the whole state of Rhode Island, way back at the beginning of our country.

In the brochures that Dad grabbed at the Visitors Center, I read some more about Roger Williams as we rode around the park. I found out all sorts of things that I never knew, things that made a lot of sense. I learned that Roger Williams really believed in people's freedom to be whoever they want to be, to believe whatever they want to believe. Even way back in Colonial times, Rhode Island was the place to go for people who weren't accepted anywhere else. People with all different religious beliefs came here to live. Plus, Rhode Island was the first colony to declare its independence from Great Britain, just before the Revolutionary War, and Rhode Island was one of the first states to make slavery illegal.

It sounded like my home state, even way back then, was a big mix of settlers who wanted to create a truly free and independent place to live. It was a place where difference was, well, not really anything different.

It all started to make sense. Being different can be a good thing.

I thought about my classmates. Labeling everyone the way I did, now that seemed to be really wrong.

Although I didn't want to admit it to myself, when Jessie accused me of judging her, she was kind of right. In my mind, I had put her into a little Glamour Girl box, just like I put Carlos in his Smarty box, Sheila in her Sporty Girl box, and Joey in his Tough Guy box.

But then, during the Precious Things presentations, it was like all of my classmates busted their fists right through those boxes that I had shut them in. And clutched in their hands were those Precious Things that surprised me, Precious Things that didn't fit with the label I had stuck on them.

I realized that no one should take one thing about a person and blow it all out of proportion, making it the only thing the person is known for. Just like I didn't want to be known as the Girl with the Leg Braces, my classmates didn't want to be labeled either. Everyone just wanted to be recognized for *everything* that they were.

Maybe that big purple CMT streak *did* belong in the painting of me, along with all of the other colorful splashes.

I suddenly knew exactly what I had to say in my campaign speech on Monday. "I need to go home!" I shouted from the backseat of the van.

Mom whipped her head around. "What? This was your idea."

"Yeah, I know, but I need to write my speech! I know what I want to say, and I've got to write it down. Quickly!"

Mom looked at Dad, who was rolling his eyes and slowly turning the steering wheel. "Told you, hon. I knew the kids would get bored with this."

"Shush," she told him and pushed his shoulder with her hand. "All right, Arlene, we'll head back. I just want to go by the carousel, OK? I love looking at that."

"OK, Mom, but I'm just going to be sitting here and thinking up my speech in my head."

"Yes, you do that."

PUMPING IT UP

I felt jumpy as I sat on the cafeteria floor Monday morning. This was going to be a humungous day. I had to give my campaign speech to the whole school that morning, and in the afternoon everyone would vote for SGA officers. This was it. All those days of campaigning, fighting battles, trying to prove myself—it all came down to today. My legs bounced in their braces, and I looked around at the kids gathering in bunches, waiting for the morning bell. I didn't see Jessie anywhere, thank goodness. I hoped to avoid her until I made it through the morning.

Just moments earlier, the boys and girls of Room 22 called a truce. Byron had admitted to me, as we walked into the cafeteria, that the boys planned to "lay low." They didn't want to risk getting into any more trouble right before the big vote. I told him that the girls felt the same way. I told Sheila how the boys felt, and Byron told Joey how the girls felt, and then Sheila and Joey shook hands while we all gathered around them on the cafeteria floor.

That's how you stop a war without losing.

The atmosphere at school sure felt different after that. It was like those commercials where the lady sprays an air freshener around a room, then takes a big whiff and smiles like she's in paradise. Yup, it was a brand new day at Greenwood. Boys and girls once again occupied the cubby room at the same time, and children of both genders were again drinking from the same bubbler. Ketchup and Mustard, feeling the peaceful vibe in the air and happy to be safe at home in their cage, jumped and hopped and dug into their bedding with joy.

The morning flowed smoothly, and soon it was time for the SGA election campaign speeches. We were called down to the auditorium one class at a time. Then I left my class and went backstage, where I waited with the other candidates.

I was feeling a little nervous at this point, but still, I was confident about what I was going to say. I had practiced my speech with Mom last night. I felt her pride stirring inside of me as I waited to be called to the stage.

After all, this was me: Arlene on the Scene. Awesome purple leg braces and much, much more. Not like everyone else. Just like me.

The audience got quiet as Mr. Musgrove strode to the podium on the stage. A big spotlight shined right on him while the rest of the room was dark. He pushed the microphone up slightly and cleared his throat.

"Good morning, students!"

People murmured, "Good morning," I think, but it was hard to tell. Mr. Musgrove continued, like he didn't care whether anyone greeted him or not.

"All right, everyone, you will be voting for your chosen SGA candidates this afternoon. We want to make sure everyone hears from each of the candidates so that you can choose wisely when you vote. Remember, voting is an important responsibility. Take it seriously. Listen to these fine students closely and make a thoughtful choice.

"All right then, we always start with the youngest candidate first. This year, we have two of the youngest candidates in Greenwood Elementary School history. We are all very proud of their efforts, especially our first speaker, who has overcome great odds to participate in this election."

Hey, what was Musgrove saying? I didn't "overcome" any greater odds than Carlos to be in this election. Things would have to change after today. No more sympathy for no reason!

"Please welcome Arlene Harper to the stage!"

Kids clapped. A big smile blasted its way onto my face. As I stepped out onto the stage, I was that performer again, like when I did the PTA speeches. I felt like I could do almost anything.

I stepped behind the podium and faced . . . the back of the podium.

Yeah, OK, I was going to need a stepstool or something.

Ms. Merrily ran out and placed a big block behind the podium. I reached out for her hand to steady myself and then stepped up. Ah, much better.

.

I dragged the microphone down to the level of my mouth, squinted out at the audience, and raised my hand high to wave at the crowd.

"Hello, fellow Greenwood people." I said firmly into the microphone. My voice boomed through the auditorium. I felt big. I felt powerful. I could be the next SGA secretary. Kids cheered and clapped.

"First, I want to thank Mr. Musgrove for giving me the chance to be up here, to be making a speech, and to be running for SGA. Bending the rules once in a while is probably a good thing."

I smiled at Mr. Musgrove and tried to make my eye wink. (I wish I could learn to do that. It would be so handy.) Mr. Musgrove wasn't smiling, though. He looked almost a little angry. Probably didn't like that "bending rules" comment. Anyway, I continued. "My fellow classmates, as an SGA officer, I will represent the values of this school. These values are learning, growing, and having fun. And most importantly, we'll be doing these things together.

"Here at Greenwood, we are one team, one big bunch of grapes, but all different shapes and sizes. We are a team of individuals, and the differences among us are good. They're not something that should split us up. They are what bands us together.

"Each of us is made up of so many cool things, and we as a school should open our arms to everyone. We should invite everyone to join in, to participate, and to make this school the best it can be.

"I know, maybe this is more than an SGA secretary is supposed do. But I want you to know what I'm about. This is what I believe. This is who I am.

"Just look at me. I have awesome purple leg braces decorated with butterflies. But I'm so much more than that Girl with the Leg Braces. And I know that each one of you is much more than you appear to be at first glance. I want to get to know everyone. And together, as one awesome team, we can learn, grow, and have fun.

"So I ask that you think about voting for me. I'm Arlene. And I'm on the scene.

"Are you with me?"

I raised my fist into the air and stared at the ceiling. I heard a few claps.

Uh-oh. My speech made no sense to anyone but me. I stared out at the dark, silent auditorium.

There was nothing left to do but try again. Maybe the audience didn't hear me.

I cleared my throat. "Are you *with* me?" I punched the air again, really hard this time. I almost knocked myself over.

I heard some more claps, then more, and then even more. The crowd flew to their feet and cheered. I held both fists high.

This right here, this was my best shot. It was all I could do.

WHAT'S INSIDE

I flew back to class and floated through the rest of
my day. I loved giving that speech, and I felt proud
of what I had said. I really believed it. I looked at
my classmates in a whole new way, and I think they
looked at me differently too.

After school, as I walked toward the bus, kids kept
coming up to me, patting me on the back and con-
gratulating me. I almost got knocked over, *again.*

Joey said, "Yo, Arlene, good talk, all that stuff
about differences. My gramps always said, 'You're
only as strong as your weakest link.' That's an army
saying. It means the strong soldiers have to help the
weak ones."

"Who are you calling weak, Joey?" I punched him lightly on the arm.

He put both fists in the air in front of me. "Better watch it, Arlene," he said with a grin. "I'm as tough as my gramps!"

"But *I* know kung fu!" Carlos said as he jumped in between Joey and me. He didn't have his fists raised, but he had his hands out in his best Jackie Chan pose.

Joey laughed loudly and said, "Oh, yeah!" He jumped on Carlos' back, but Carlos kept walking, basically giving Joey a piggyback ride.

"See?" Carlos shouted. "I'll carry the weak ones to the transport vehicles. Because I am the strongest one of all! Oh, hey, good speech, Arlene!"

"You too, Carlos!" I called, as he wobbled with his heavy load toward the buses.

"Hey, Arlene! Arlene! Hey! Arlene!" It was Byron. "That speech was sooo good! How did you think all that stuff up? Weren't you nervous up there? I think you're going to win, I really do. Will you give me a job with SGA? Can I have extra hall passes, huh?"

"Bryon, thanks," I said. "But I told you before, I'm just running for secretary. I don't get extra hall passes."

"No," Byron said, "I heard that people were going to write you in as president!"

"That's crazy talk," I said. "That'll never happen."

Byron shrugged and ran to catch up with the other boys.

I continued toward my bus. But then I looked up and saw that Jessie was about to cross my path. I stopped. Just like with a black cat, I figured this had to be bad luck.

Jessie stopped right in front of me. "Do I look like a black cat to you?"

"No."

"Then what'd you stop for?"

I shrugged. The two of us stewed in an awkward silence for a moment.

Jessie sighed like she was all frustrated, like some invisible force was making her talk to me. "Your speech was pretty good. You're probably going to win, you know. You're just so *popular.*" She said that last word with a nasal whine, like popularity was a bad thing in a school-wide election.

"Thanks, I think." Now what? I searched for something neutral to say. No need to get in another big fight with this girl now. I was feeling too good. "But we won't really know who's going to win until tomorrow."

"Look, Harper. Let's not pretend we're best friends here. But . . ." Jessie stared at the ground as she made dirt circles with the tip of her shoe. "But, look, I know I was out of line telling you that you couldn't hack it, being in the election. You proved that you can do just about anything you want. I was just upset, that's all. I mean, you came back to school this year and everybody loved you, everybody paid so much attention to you. And you let that all happen, sometimes even when it was just because people were feeling sorry for you. Then you kept acting as if you were just like everybody else. But you're not."

Was this supposed to be an apology? I lowered my head slightly and sneaked a peek at Jessie's face. She still had her head bent way down and was watching her sneaker dig what was now a huge hole. I saw her eyes blinking quickly as she sniffled and turned away from me.

I finally realized what was making Jessie act so mean. She *was* jealous. Before I came on the scene, she was certainly the most popular girl in our grade, if not the whole school. Maybe I messed that up when my campaign started to really work.

"Jessie, I was just doing the best I could do in the election. I didn't expect all this to happen."

Jessie turned back toward me and raised her head. Any trace of tears was gone. She touched her ponytail lightly with her hand but didn't take her scrunchie out. She looked a little sad.

So I kept talking. "Listen, you were a little right about me too. I was judging you, thinking you were just into fashion and glamour. I mean, I had no idea that you liked sports. I had no idea about all the other kids either, that Carlos was into kung fu or that Sheila could play the cello. Maybe we all learned something this year, that what you see on the outside of a person isn't all that there is."

Jessie looked right at me. "I'm not as mean as you think, you know," she said quietly.

"I know, Jessie. I know." Just then, a flash of a good idea popped into my brain. "Maybe it's time that you and I called a truce," I offered.

Jessie thought this over for a minute and looked to the ground again. "I don't have to pretend that

I really like you, do I?" Then she raised her eyes to me and smirked slightly, like she wanted to keep me guessing about whether she was joking or for real.

Without missing a beat I answered, "No, as long as I don't have to pretend to like you."

"Deal."

We shook hands on our agreement to not like each other, and then we walked away in opposite directions.

I climbed the steps onto my bus and found a seat way in back. I couldn't believe it. All that stuff from Jessie felt so mean, and it turned out to be just a cover-up. Deep down, Jessie was worried about what people thought of her too.

Whoa, did Jessie and I have something in common?

THE ELECTION!

The next day, the morning announcements were going to reveal the winners of the election. Mom had sent me off to school with a big kiss. "Good luck, sweetie! No matter what happens, we're all so proud of you!"

In the classroom, I threw my coat and book bag in the direction of my hook in the cubby room. Whatever. Who cared. Time needed to move faster! I sat down on the edge of my seat and wiggled and bounced, trying to speed up the clock so that the morning announcements could begin.

Finally they came on. "Good morning, Greenwood students," said some sixth grader. The sixth graders got to do the announcements every morning. Maybe I'll try out for *that* job when I get to the sixth grade. (Hey, maybe I'll try out for it in the fifth grade!) Of course, I might have to change the name to *Morning Rap with Arlene Harper.*

"Get ready," the announcer said, "because the election results are *in*! This was a record-breaking election, with the youngest candidates ever, and the most voter participation. Way to go, Greenwood!

"For secretary, surprisingly enough, one of our youngest candidates pulled ahead of the competition, including a fifth grader. Announcing, as secretary of the SGA, Carlos Martinez!"

Huh. OK, well, I had done my best. It was all I could do. The boys erupted in cheers. Even a lot of the girls congratulated Carlos. They were really glad that a fourth grader had shown Mr. Musgrove that we deserved to be in the elections. I waved at Carlos and smiled. "Nice going," I mouthed. His eyes were squeezed almost shut under the pressure of his tremendous smile. "Thanks!" he called.

I didn't feel bad, really. I was proud that I had come this far. Most of all, I was happy with all I had learned, about my classmates and about myself.

The announcer continued, telling us that some sixth grader won treasurer. I thought about next year. Maybe I'd have a better chance at treasurer. "For president," the announcer said, "we have a surprising result. For the first time ever, a write-in candidate earned the most votes."

What?

"Our new SGA president is . . ."

Could Byron have been right?

". . . Arlene Harper!"

This time the whole class erupted together like a big volcano. They stood up, cried out, and cheered. I had won! I couldn't believe it. I tried to swallow the news that not only did I win the election, I was president!

I hugged Lauren and Byron and all my friends. They seemed so happy for me. I went over to Sheila and gave her a big high five. She picked me up into the air.

OK, that was a little dangerous. I gripped her shoulders tightly until she put me down, but I managed to keep smiling. At least my feet were on the floor again.

Ms. Merrily tried to calm us down, but it was useless, so she let us cheer for a little while longer.

What a frenzy! What a feeling! Even the boys were happy, for the most part. Carlos gave me a high ten, and Spencer congratulated me on a hard-fought campaign. He said he hoped I wasn't mad at his attempts to sabotage me with taco grease. "No worries, Spence," I said. "It's all in the game."

Jessie walked over to me slowly, awkwardly, as the kids bounced around us. "Nice job, Arlene. You did it. Guess you are just like everyone else."

"Nah, I'm just me, doing my best. It's all I can do."

"But really, though. Good job."

"Thanks, Jessie."

And then she walked away. I thought both of us were a little relieved to have gotten that conversation over with.

She was a tough one, that Jessie. Despite my promise to her yesterday, I was actually starting to like her.

I finally got to do my Precious Things presentation, a week late. I brought in the Claude Monet poster that hangs in my room. I told the class that each one of us is like this painting, made up of lots of different colored strokes. And when you put all these little pieces together, they make a big, beautiful whole.

I explained that Room 22 is like this too, and so is Greenwood Elementary School, Rhode Island, and really, the whole world. When you get lots of different kinds of people together, they can create one awesome picture.

And I told the class that this painting is precious for all of these reasons, but mostly because it was given to me by a person most precious to me: my mother.

GET READY

It was one fantastic year, the fourth grade. I did a great job as president of SGA, if I do say so myself. We made new cafeteria rules (no grease collecting), new rules about SGA officers (anyone who can meet the requirements of the essay, the meetings, the speech, etc. is eligible to run for office), new rules for recess (no leaf throwing or rock collecting), and new rules about classroom pets (fish only).

We also made things easier around the school for people like Mom and me, people who have a disability. I've heard these kinds of changes are called making things more "accessible," and boy, is it fantastic! Mr. Peterson removed two seats right near the stage in the auditorium so Mom can finally have a decent view. And he also built ramps over all those pesky steps in the hallways. Mr. Musgrove even agreed to have a committee look into whether the bathrooms could be made more accessible. Personally, I'd be happy if they simply keep them stocked with paper towels so that I don't have to always wipe my hands on my pants. But it's awesome that they're taking accessibility seriously.

Even the kids at school had a new attitude. We weren't all stuck in separate groups anymore. Carlos and Joey and Spencer all played together sometimes. Lauren could be found playing with Sheila or even Jessie. And people really got to know what I'm about. I'm not some girl with leg braces who you should feel sorry for. I'm a poet, a pal, a president.

There was one last thing I felt I had to do before I finished fourth grade, and that was have another heart-to-heart with Mr. Musgrove. I called his secretary and made an appointment with him.

When I entered his office, he looked at me, looked at the schedule on his desk, and looked at me again. This time he also looked at the calendar, like he had lost track of time and was repeating events in his life by mistake.

"Mr. Musgrove," I began. "It's me, here to see you again. I just want to thank you for giving me a chance in the elections."

He leaned back and smiled.

"I'm glad it worked out. Congratulations on a great presidency." Mr. Musgrove paused. "I will admit, Arlene, that I didn't quite believe you could do it."

"I know," I said. "A lot of people look at me and they decide things, like about what I can do. But you can't let one part of a person cover up everything else."

"That is indeed true, Arlene." He sighed, and his face wrinkles smoothed out a little. "It's been a pleasure working with you this year, young lady. I look forward to working with you again next year."

He reached over to shake my hand.

"You'd better get ready!" I said with a smirk.

Mr. Musgrove's wrinkles came back, especially on his forehead.

Oops. I went too far.

Well, I figure I better start planning over the summer. Now that I put it out there, I need to have something really big in store for the fifth grade!

Note To Readers

Charcot-Marie-Tooth, or CMT as Arlene says, is a complicated sounding disease. And it affects a lot of people, about 2.6 million around the world. It is the most common nerve disorder that can be

The real people behind the story: Marybeth Sidoti Caldarone and her daughter, Grace

passed down within families, although as Arlene points out, it's not always passed down. Sometimes it just shows up without anyone else in the family having it.

There are many different types of CMT, too, and it can affect kids and adults in lots of different ways. Someone in your community might be living with CMT, and you might not even realize it.

In fact, there really is a nine-year-old girl living with CMT in Rhode Island. Her name is Grace Caldarone. And yes, that's the same last name as one of the women who wrote this book! Grace's mother, Marybeth Caldarone, also has CMT, just like Arlene's mother in this book. Marybeth and Carol Liu are great friends, and Carol always thought Grace was such a cool kid that someone should write a book about her. So Carol and Marybeth did.

Now, to be completely honest, the authors made up all that stuff about Plumpy the Pumpkin, Ketchup and Mustard, and the Greenwood Elementary SGA elections. That was just for fun. But the stuff about CMT is all true.

Although scientists around the world are working hard to find new treatments and even a cure for CMT, they still have a way to go. Millions of people are hoping and praying that they may soon be able to freely move their arms and legs again. This is something that Grace Caldarone and her mom dream about a lot, and so they are working really hard to make it happen.

If you want to learn more about CMT, you can go to the Hereditary Neuropathy Foundation website, www.hnf-cure.org. If you want to learn more about Grace and her family's mission to help people living with CMT, you can visit www.gracescouragecrusade.com.

The authors hope you have enjoyed Arlene's adventures, and that you learned something about what it's like to live with a disability. As Arlene found out, we can all benefit from learning a little more about each other.

Acknowledgments

We would like to thank the many, many people who believed in and supported this book. Although impossible to name everyone here, we'd like to acknowledge specifically as many as we can. We thank J.D. Griffith of the CMT Foundation for his generous support of this project. Thank you as well to the 1ActPerDay Foundation for their grant. A special thank you to Tino and Ann Clemente, whose incredibly generous gift made it possible for us to begin publication even earlier than expected. We are also grateful to the hundreds of family members and friends who supported this book, especially RoseMarie Sidoti, Mark Sidoti, Liz Sidoti, and Ed Smith who all helped organize fundraising efforts. And to Allison Moore, Terri Eickel, Carolyn Spector, Jess Johnston, and the Board of Directors of the Hereditary Neuropathy Foundation: we obviously couldn't have done any of this without you. Thank you for your enthusiastic response to our out-of-the-blue phone call saying, hey, we've got an idea about a book!

We'd like to also thank those who helped with the writing and production of this book. We appreciate our readers for their valuable time, expertise and editorial analysis, especially Jennifer Alessi McGinley, Nadya Hosein, Bernie Magee, Gloria Benjamin, Susan Champlin, Dona Dulski, and Eugene Sidoti. A special thank you to our own children, Christopher, Jaden, Grace, and Malcolm, who all offered that kind of honest criticism you only get from your own kids. Thank you to Stan Mack for his guidance and calm consultation throughout this process. Thanks also to Skyler Calandro for capturing Arlene's spirit in that first illustration. We are especially grateful to Mark Minnig for the many hours and much talent he contributed for the cover illustration. Finally, we have tremendous appreciation for all of the advice and support from the folks at Greenleaf Book Group.

And to our ever-enduring husbands: we couldn't have done any of this without you!

About the Authors

Carol grew up in Rhode Island, enjoying coffee milk and ignoring R's in words—until she met Marybeth, a New Yorker who was studying to be a speech therapist at the University of Rhode Island. Marybeth first fixed Carol's speech, and then they became best friends. They wrote this book to help find a cure for Charcot-Marie-Tooth (CMT) disease, which affects both Marybeth and her daughter, Grace. All proceeds will be donated to help those living with CMT.

Carol Liu is an attorney and clinical social worker working with children who have special needs in the Washington, DC area. She is also the co-author of *True Friends*, a children's picture book.

Marybeth Sidoti Caldarone is a speech/language pathologist helping children in public schools in southern Rhode Island. She is actively involved in the network of organizations committed to finding a cure for CMT.